STREAMER

SUE-ELLEN PASHLEY

2ND EDITION

Copyright © Sue-Ellen Pashley 2015

All rights reserved. No part of this book may be reproduced or transmitted in any form or by any means, electronic or mechanical, including photocopying, recording or by any information storage and retrieval system, without prior permission in writing from the publisher.

National Library of Australia cataloguing-in-publication data:
Pashley, Sue-Ellen

Paperback ISBN 978-0-6488018-3-2

The characters and events in this book are fictitious and any resemblance to real persons, living or dead, is purely coincidental.

Printed in Australia by Ingram Spark
Cover design by Betibup33

Second Edition

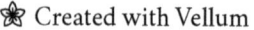 Created with Vellum

CHAPTER 1

I have no idea where I am.
But the seat under me is hard.
Solid.

I grab the table top with shaking hands, holding it so tightly my fingers turn white under the pressure. Not that that's going to stop me from disappearing.

Again.

I'm in a coffee shop. That's all I know. Not where it is. Not how I got here. Not when I'm going to leave.

I take a deep breath. It's shaky and I have to take another and then another before I begin to breathe properly. I want to gasp the air in, suck it into my body, but there are people all around me and I don't need to attract attention. So I'm controlled. Outwardly anyway.

The smell of real coffee swirls in the air, making my stomach roll, and there are the obligatory cakes and pastries in the glass cabinet. The chink of teaspoons against china sets my nerves on edge as the chatter of people who have something to say to each other surrounds me, inundates me, overwhelms me. I take another breath.

I have no sense that I've been here before, no vague feeling of knowing where I am. Nothing that gives me any clues.

I look around at the surrounding tables, trying not to be too obvious, waiting for that moment when I make a connection with someone, that moment when I'm noticed. I almost don't want to and have to fight the urge to just keep my eyes on the non-descript laminated table top. Because I know that as soon as someone recognises me, I'll no longer be here. I'll be somewhere else. Somewhere just as unfamiliar. That's what's happened over the last forty-eight hours anyway.

The waitress comes to my table. She doesn't seem surprised that I'm here but then, no one has been. I appear out of mid-air and no one seems to even notice. I don't know how that's possible. But then I don't know how any of this is possible. In fact, there is so much I don't know it makes me feel nauseous. Simple things like why is this happening, what's causing it, how do I stop it, what's my name...?

I look up at her but there's no recognition in her

eyes. Nothing that says she knows me, that I'm a regular, that I have a coffee fixation…

'What can I get you?'

'Just coffee. A cappuccino.' Not that I'll probably get a chance to drink it but it seems the right thing to do when I'm going to sit at one of her tables for god knows how long.

She nods and goes to move off.

'Umm…excuse me.'

She turns back and raises her eyebrows. Waiting.

'Have I been here before? I mean, have you seen me in here before today?'

It probably sounds like a stupid question but I need to ask. I hold myself still, waiting for her answer, even though my heart is thumping out an erratic rhythm in my chest, like Morse code for the panic that's just waiting to take hold. Waiting to see if there's something I can work with before it kicks in. Some indicator of who I am...

She frowns at me, like she's worried about my mental stability, and then shakes her head.

'I don't think so.'

I slump back in the chair and she shoots me one last confused look before leaving. I don't blame her – I'd want to get away from me too – this weird girl who sits in her café and doesn't know if she's been here before. I shut my eyes, rubbing them with my fingers, trying to make my brain work. But my memories are blank, like a computer wiped clean.

All I have are vague…feelings…about a handful of the locations I've been turning up in over the last two days. Like I might have been there before.

Maybe…

But it's like the knowledge is just out of reach, hiding in the shadows every time I get close. As far as I can tell, I've just been going from one place to the next without any rhyme or reason. Or not one that I can work out anyway. And I should be tired after forty-eight hours of no sleep. I don't know how I'm not. Something else I can add to the list of things I need answers to.

I put my forehead on the table, smelling the cleaning solution they use between patrons. My head hurts with it all…my brain feels like it's pulsing, straining, ready to explode at any moment – brains all over the table in one giant, squelchy mess. That'd be something to look forward to.

I swallow the slightly hysterical bubble of laughter that's trying to force its way out.

It's too much; too overwhelming confusing and hard and wrong. And the thought of going on like this – never resting, never stopping, never knowing…always alone, fills me with a dread that sinks into me, like it's weakening my bones, making me less somehow. I can't do it. I can't!

Tears form in my eyes and for a second, I contemplate letting them fall, giving into them. But if I do, I'll be lost. Melting away with them.

I sit up again and take a deep breath, pushing the anxiety down as far as I can, and run my fingers through my hair – short and dark. I know this from when I looked in the mirror yesterday. Even though my reflection didn't give me any clues either – just a vague feeling of having seen it before. How can you look in a mirror and not recognise yourself, for God's sake?

The waitress puts the coffee in front of me, stumbling a little as she does so that dribbles of brown cascade over the white cup.

'Sorry. I don't know what's wrong with me.'

I smile - it's only a small tilt of my lips but it's all I can muster - just wanting her to go away now. Which proves how messed up I am. I don't want to be alone but I don't want company either. Well, not the company of strangers anyway.

I set the cup handle parallel to the table edge, needing the order it creates - the only thing I feel like I can control at the moment - and move the spoon through the froth before putting it in my mouth, letting the bubbles melt on my tongue.

That's when I look up and see her, through the people standing at the counter, sitting at a table by herself in the corner. I know her. Even though I don't know how and I don't know who she is, I know she has a connection with me.

And then she looks up.

There's a moment of surprise on her face – a

reaction that says she knows me too – and then she's standing, her face serious, moving towards me. I hold on to the table, wanting to keep myself here, needing her to tell me who I am but it's no good.

I am gone.

CHAPTER 2

I put my hand out as I stumble, leaning against the wall to stop myself falling. I'm in a house.

I close my eyes, squeezing them tight, tight, tight. Trying with everything that's in me to go back to the café. Willing my body to just do it. To go back. Talk to the woman. Go, go, go. I hold my breath and open my eyes.

I'm still in the house.

My body sags and I put one hand on my knee to stop myself falling to the ground, sucking in air, trying to breathe past the lump that's formed in my throat.

What is this? Why does it keep happening? And why to me? What have I done that I'm being punished like this?

Standing again, I grip the wall and shake my

head. Why do I even bother asking that question over and over? There's no point. I need to find answers, not keep on whining that it isn't fair. It isn't. That's all there is to it. Get a grip. Move on. Look for information.

I let go of the wall.

The late afternoon sun is shining softly through the blinds in the window. It feels familiar…enough to know I've been here before, even if I can't remember when or why.

It's a lounge room. The grey carpet is worn under my feet, parts of the weave showing through like a bald man with a comb over, and the furniture looks old and stained, as if the owner stopped caring a long time ago. The whole place looks like that – like someone used to care but hasn't been bothered for years. And there's a musty smell in the air, as if the windows haven't been opened for a while. That's when it suddenly occurs to me that I may not be alone.

'Hello?'

The quietness presses in.

'Is anyone home?'

Again, no answer. I don't know if that's good or bad. To actually have someone to talk to – someone who knows me – would be beyond fantastic. But I probably wouldn't get the chance to ask them anything before I disappeared anyway. Better to look around before whoever lives here comes back.

The bookcase beside me is packed full; books stuffed in at different angles where their owner has tried to make them all fit. I run my finger over the spines. Everything from biographies to novels to non-fiction, all crammed in together with no organisation. None that I can see anyway.

There's a well-used copy of 'Little Women', the spine cracking with age and love, and I take it out, opening the front cover. There's an inscription.

'To Jennifer, with love, Mum and Dad.'

Jennifer. The name strikes a chord for me, way down in my stomach. I know that name. It's important to me.

I physically ache with all that I don't know, like my head is sick of the pain of trying to remember and has decided to share it with the rest of my body. Putting the book on a coffee table, I look around the room, in a hurry now. It feels like the first real connection. The first of something that makes sense.

There are photos on a shelf at the other end of the room and I hurry over, worried suddenly, that someone will arrive home before I get to look at them. They're crowded together in a collage of different times and places and I settle on one at the front in a tarnished silver frame. There are three people. The girl at the front looks enough like me that I'm sure it is. She…I…she looks to be about ten. The hair is longer, down to the middle of her back but the grey-green eyes are the same. It must be me.

I want it to be. So badly that my chest is tight with the possibility.

The woman at the back has dark hair too, cropped short like mine is now. She's staring at the camera, the ghost of a smile on her face, her hands on each of the shoulders of the children like she's trying to keep them in place.

Jennifer. My mother.

That thought pops into my head so suddenly that I put my hand over my mouth, trying to stifle a sob, keeping it in so it doesn't encourage others to follow. I don't have time to cry. Not when I'm starting to get answers. Because she is a part of me – a part of my life. I'm sure of it. A little piece has slid back into place, even if I can't remember any details.

It's a start.

A connection.

I'm not lost.

My eyes slide to the other person in the photo. A boy. Teenager. Probably somewhere around sixteen or seventeen. Verging on manhood but still a boy. My heart starts to thump as I look at him and my mouth is suddenly dry. There's something… wrong. It's the only way I can describe it. Like there's something I desperately need to do. Something big. Now. Right now.

I start to pace, tapping my finger on the frame. Adrenalin is shooting through my body like it's trying to replace my blood. Christ, why do I feel like this? It seems like my body knows there's something important even if my head can't remember. I chew the pad of my thumb, trying to force something – a name, a connection – anything!

'Fuck. Fuck. Fuck.'

It doesn't help. I look more closely at the photo, like it's going to tell me something. He's not smiling and I wonder why. Whether he was angry at that point in time or if he's just not a smiler. Serious. Somehow that feels like it fits. My brother? He must be. I scan the other photos on the table. Most of them are of me. I think they are anyway. A few though, are of this boy, unsmiling in all of them except one where I think he must be about three. What is it that's made him so solemn?

I turn the frame over, spinning the little plastic locks that hold the cover in place. My fingers tremble and it takes three attempts to move the last one before I reef open the fabric covered back, almost tearing it off. There's nothing written on the back of the photo but it doesn't matter. I take it out, looking at it for a moment longer before folding it and putting it in the pocket of my shorts. Hopefully it will come with me when I go. Because I know, sooner or later, whether I want to or not, I'll be gone from here.

I look around again, wondering if this is still my home or if I've moved out. Wondering what other bits of my life are here. I go out into the hall area and then stop to get my bearings. A kitchen is at the back of the house and there's a staircase at the front. I make my way towards the stairs. To a bedroom maybe. A room with memories of my life.

I'm only halfway down the hall when I hear a key in the front door. I freeze. There's nowhere to go. Nowhere to hide until I can make it upstairs. I want to scream. I'm so close. But then the door is opening and she's standing there, looking older than the photo. And gaunter, like she hasn't eaten for days. But it's still her.

Jennifer. My mother.

The shock on her face is easy to see and she stands totally still for a second, mirroring me. Then her hand goes up to the doorframe, as if she's using it to hold herself up.

'What are you doing here?'

'Mum?'

And that's all I get the chance to say. I watch her face harden, eyes narrowed, before I'm swept away again.

CHAPTER 3

I land on my hands and knees on a jetty. The wood is rough under my fingers. Old and weathered and starting to splinter. Just what my soul feels like. I sit up, looking around me, gasping for air again. I'm the only one here. Just me and the moon, coming up over the water. Alone again.

I'm back to vague recollections. I've been here at some stage in a past I can't remember. Been here and done something. Swam maybe. Or fished. But at this moment, I don't care why this place is familiar. I'm sick of it. Sick of trying to make sense of it all when there is nothing in my head to help.

I lie on my back on the unforgiving wood and look up at the stars.

I want my Mum.

I want to go back and be with her and get held in her arms. Not that she really looked like the type of woman that'd be into hugs, but I don't care. I just want to be with someone who knows me. Someone who could help. I wrap my own arms around body instead. They're a cold substitute.

The tears I denied myself in the café start to come, rolling from my eyes, down the sides of my face, dripping onto the wood which has already seen so much salty water that my tears are hardly going to make a difference. I don't even attempt to wipe them away.

And then I'm sobbing, big ones that come from my gut, jerking out of me so hard I can't lie on my back anymore. I roll on my side, bringing my knees to my chest and let them come.

I cry for all of it – the life I can't remember and the hugs I can't get and the brother who doesn't seem to smile. Sob until it's all gone and then I just lay there, staring into the darkness, wanting this random zapping to stop. I can't keep doing it.

I only stir when the first slivers of sun touch me. Sunrise. My eyes are gritty and I rub at them, even if it doesn't help. Sitting up, my body is stiff and sore. I stretch, blinking at the early light, and attempt to stand.

And then I'm not there anymore.

CHAPTER 4

I'm in an apartment. A small one. Still darkened to the new day by the window coverings. It's familiar but I don't think it's mine. It's too brown for one thing. In the little bit of light sneaking under the blinds I can see a brown couch and a brown table and a brown mat. Definitely not mine. How is it I can't remember my goddamn name but I know I like colour and light? Stupid!

I turn in a circle, looking around me. I see a bedroom through an open door. A person maybe. Someone else who might know me.

Tiptoeing over, trying to make sure the wooden floor doesn't squeak and give me away, I stop at the door frame, holding on. The light from a computer screen on the desk near the bed gives me enough light to see.

There's a man in the bed. A beautiful man.

Asleep. The covers have been pushed down, leaving the top half of him uncovered. Naked. He has one arm up over his head, the other hand resting on his chest. His hair – blond, I think, although it's hard to tell in the half dark – is tousled from sleep. The muscles in his arms and chest are easy to see, even in rest.

I step into the room, wanting to be closer, and only stop when I'm next to him, the bed frame pushing into my shins. It feels like this physical barrier is the only thing stopping me from climbing under the sheets with him. Christ!

I want to touch him so badly I have to clench my fingers together in front of me to stop myself.

I want him.

There's no denying it. Everything in me clenches at the thought of putting my lips on his, tasting him, pushing my fingers through his hair and over his skin, moving the covers further down…

I take a deep, shuddering breath, trying to get control. Because however much my body wants him, he's a stranger. A cute stranger, sure, but still an unknown. How can he be having this effect on me when I don't know who he is?

Before I give into the urge to bend down and run my fingertips down his chest, using his muscles as a road map to the edge of the sheet and then under it, I take a step back, bumping into the chair behind me. It rattles in protest and I freeze, holding my breath, watching him as he opens his eyes, blinking away the fogginess of sleep. Waiting for him to see me. To recognise me.

He frowns for a second and then his eyes widen. He jerks up onto his elbow.

'Rhiannon?' He reaches out a hand to me. 'Rhi, don't go! Stay here!'

But I don't know how to do that. I want to ask him to help me but it's too late.

CHAPTER 5

I'm at a lookout, high on top of a cliff, surrounded by a safety fence. The ocean stretches out in front of me, so bright blue in the early morning light that I have to shade my eyes, and the salt spray lingers in the air as waves break below. I was here on the first day of this insane zapping experience, which is something new. I've never been back to the same place twice.

The difference now is I know something else. I know I've been here with him. The man in the bed. The man that gave me my name.

Rhiannon. Rhi.

It fits, like a small piece of china in a broken cup. I'm starting to glue myself back together.

I sit on the wooden seat, looking out over the ever-moving water, trying to keep my mind blank, just in case something else comes back. Some other memory that will give me more clues. I have a name, a family and obviously some connection to the man in the bed. Especially since he seemed to understand something about my disappearing trick.

I think again about how much I wanted to touch him, kiss him, taste him, and feel my cheeks burning. I wonder if I felt like that because I've touched him before and some sub-conscious part of me has missed it or because I've always wanted to and never got the chance. I put my fingers to my lips, imagining his there, his hand on my back, pulling me closer…

I shake my head. I'm supposed to be trying to remember things, not make things up, no matter how delicious they might be.

The seat shakes slightly and I whip my head around. There's a man sitting on the other end of the bench – middle age, fit, tall, skin tanned to the point of looking leathery. He's smiling at me but I don't have that familiar feeling with him. And I'm not disappearing. I'm fairly certain this means I haven't met him before.

'It's a lovely morning for it.'

I nod, wondering what he wants. Is it normal that my thoughts have gone straight there? He could just be up for a chat, for God's sake. Why did I automatically think he would want more than that? Not that I really want to be talking. I'd rather be with the few memories I have so I can toss them around in my head like a sparse green salad.

'Looks like we're the only souls brave enough to be out this early. But this is the best time of the day, don't you think? When you can appreciate the true beauty of mother nature. That light on the ocean, the smell of the sea. It's amazing.'

'Yes.'

He shifts in the seat, turning his body towards me while stretching his leg out. His arm goes along the back of the seat, closer towards me. Not touching but in my space. I hunch forward, moving away from him, my body vibrating with tension, on high alert, even though I don't know why. I've never met this man. I know nothing about him – and all he's done is talk to me. And yet…there's something else. Something that makes me uncomfortable. Or maybe I'm a paranoid person by nature. Maybe that's part of who I am. My left leg starts to jiggle.

'Are you from around here?'

I don't know. That's what I should say.

'No.' It's easier.

'So what, just visiting family and friends then?'

Shut up, shut up! Go away!

'No.'

'All alone hey, just like me.'

I turn slightly to face him. He's still smiling but there's something behind his words now. Something…off. I grip the edge of the seat, my legs tense. I want to leave. To run. But he is between me and the exit. Where's the frigging zapping thing when I need it?

'Not really, I'm meeting someone for breakfast. In fact, I'd better go.'

I rise up as smoothly as I can, trying not to show that my heart's beating as fast as a hummingbird's wings. Trying to look calm rather than like I'm about to explode from the adrenaline rushing through me. He grabs my hand as I pass.

'Now don't rush off. I don't think you're meeting anyone at all. I think you're lying to me. Why would you do that?'

I try to pull away but he is too strong. And big. My hand's engulfed by his. I try to prise his fingers away but I may as well be trying to twist steel. He laughs and jerks me in so quickly I land on his lap.

A squeak emits from my mouth – a bloody squeak! – and he laughs again.

'Such a little thing. And you sound like a mouse too. You and I could have some fun this morning. Don't you think that's a good idea?'

He runs his hand up the inside of my thigh, his skin on mine. Touching me. His fingers on the edge of my shorts and then under them. I struggle, dragging his hand away, but I can't get free with his other hand wrapped like a vice around my waist.

'Stop it. Let me go!'

He pushes his hand up under my shirt and grabs

my breast, his nails sharp even through my bra, hurting me, and I shove his hand away again.

'Stop it! Fucking pervert! Get away from me!'

I pound at him with my fist, hitting his jaw, his chest – anywhere I can make contact – but he laughs again, only stopping when I try to bite him. He brings his hand up and slaps my face. Hard enough that my ear rings and I can taste blood on the inside of my cheek. He grabs hold of my jaw and pulls my head around, bringing my lips to his. I can feel his tongue in my mouth. His tongue! I jerk back but there's only so far I can go in his grip.

No, no, no, this can't be happening. Not to me!

He laughs.

And that's when it happens.

I don't know how and I'm not even sure that I'm actually doing it but suddenly, he goes rigid. His eyes are wide, like his eyeballs are straining to pop out, and he is gasping for breath like a fish on the sand. His hand drops away from me and he grips the bench, leaning back as if he's trying to make more room in his chest. And when he looks at me, I can see his fear, his shock, and for a moment, I'm glad of it.

I can feel him – his life force or his energy or whatever you want to call it, pouring into me, filling me up. It's nourishing. More than that – it's invigorating. And I want it. All of it. I want to drain it from him and use it for myself, even if I don't know what this really is. Even if I don't know how I'm doing it.

I want it.

It's only when he falls over sideways on the seat, his head hitting the seat with a loud thump in the quiet of the morning, that I jump away from him and it stops, like a broken connection. It's only then that I come back to my senses. Come back to reality. And I cover my mouth in horror, unable to understand what's happened.

What the hell have I done? What am I, for God's sake?

He is grey – his lips, his face – everything is grey. Except for his eyes, which are open and staring. They're no longer full of fear or shock. They're no longer full of anything. Blank. As if he's dead. Jesus Christ, I've killed him!

I stumble back, feeling the fence at my back, gripping on to it like it's the only thing keeping me standing. I can't breathe. Can't think. I don't know what to do.

I've killed him. Killed him! Fuck!

I jerk my head around, looking for witnesses but it's still just me and him.

The person I've murdered.

Panic threatens to swamp me, drown me, and I hold the fence tighter, feeling the wire cut into my skin. It helps me to focus. Enough to realise I can't contact anyone without a phone. And that there's no way I'm touching him. I can't bring myself to do that. Even if that makes me a horrible person.

So I turn and run.

Run like something is chasing me. But I don't even reach the end of the fenced area before I'm gone.

CHAPTER 6

I suck in a lung full of air and then cough, trying not to throw up. The woman on the train next to me moves away slightly, like I might infect her. Probably a smart move considering I've just killed someone. At least, I'm pretty sure I have. He looked dead. Dead, dead, dead. The word echoes in my brain. All I can see is him lying on the seat, eyes open, unblinking. The image burned into my brain. I suck in another breath and try to stop the shaking that's taking over my body.

I can't sit still, so I get up and pace instead. Up and down, up and down, swaying to the movement of the train, hanging onto the handles on the seats as I go. No one really takes any notice of me. Or if they do, they look away before I see them.

What does it mean that I could do that? Suck the

life out of him, like a frigging energy vampire or something. Jesus!

And I can still feel his energy in me. I'm almost buzzing with it. Which is just sick. I want it out of me, except I don't know how to do that anymore than I know how it got in me in the first place.

I should call the police. He probably has a family, even if he was a sick, perverted arsehole. Except what am I going to tell them? *Sorry officer, I don't know how I killed him, but I'm buzzing with his energy.* That'd go down well. And what if they want to lock me up and I disappear from the cell, zapping away to somewhere else. Then I'll be an escaped prisoner.

And I didn't mean to kill him. God, all I wanted to do was to get away!

I stop pacing and hold onto one of the poles near the doors, leaning my forehead against the cold metal, shutting my eyes for a moment and concentrating on my breathing, trying to focus. Trying to get a hold of myself. Trying to think about what I need to do. Which is ridiculous really since I have absolutely zero control.

That thought makes me pause. Because this last zap onto the train felt different. And not just because I was freaking out. When I stop and think about it now, I was more aware of how the zapping felt – what was happening in my body. Like the excess energy has made it more noticeable.

I wonder if that means I can control it, even enough to not disappear as soon as someone recognises me. Hope flares in me like a flamethrower being ignited.

I tap my fingers against the pole, waiting for the train to pull into the next station. If I'm going to try and work out how this zapping thing works, then I don't want to do it on something that's moving. That just adds another layer of difficulty I don't need.

There's only a few people getting off and I race up the steps from the track. I see a park over the road and I dodge people obviously heading to work, being careful not to look anyone in the face, not wanting to disappear. Not yet. Not before I've had a chance to try this out.

I stand on a patch of grass and wonder how I should start. Feeling stupid. And horrible. Am I just going to do this and not worry about the man on the bench? Leave some other poor unsuspecting, innocent person to find him? And yet, what can I do? I have no way to get back to him – I don't even know where he is to be able to tell the police, for God's sake. *He's at a cliff overlooking the water. State? Not sure. Town? Uh, no idea, sorry. General sort of area then? Near the ocean?*

I put my hands up to my cheeks, trying to think. Nothing comes to me. Nothing at all! And anyway, maybe he deserved it. Maybe I'm not the only girl he's tried that on. Maybe I've protected other women by killing him... I wince. Jesus! Justifying murder now. Awesome!

But it doesn't change the fact that there's nothing I can do.

I take a deep breath and shut my eyes, trying to focus on me and on the energy in me. The energy I took from him. I shake my head. Stop it!

I think about the movements in the energy when I zapped, how it collected in my chest like metal filings to a magnet, racing in, clumping together, before it exploded and moved me. I open my eyes again. There's a fountain a few metres away. Not too far. A good start maybe.

I focus on the energy, gently trying to move it but it ignores all my efforts, slipping away like water through my fingers. I try to force it. I even close my eyes again, focusing on its movement, using everything in me to get it to shift. Nothing. I'm still standing in the same place. The one time I actually want to move and I'm still here. Fan-frigging-tastic!

I crouch down, making myself smaller, the grass soft under my hands, and think about how much I want to move...how much I want to be over there... how much I want to control this. And my body sort of...shimmers, like it's trying to move but can't get there. Like a car engine not quite turning over. Not really what I was looking for but it's a start.

I look up from the grass to find a little girl in

front of me, staring. She has a ball in her hand and I can see her mum coming up behind her.

'Hello.'

She just stands there, looking at me. As solemn as the pictures of my brother.

'You wobbled.'

I smile at her.

'Did I?'

She nods.

'Your whole body. It wobbled, like you weren't here and then you were here again.'

My smile gets wider.

'Cool.'

'Can I do that?'

I shake my head.

'Probably not. I'm not even sure how I did it.'

She nods like this makes perfect sense. Her mother reaches us and quickly apologises before whisking her daughter away. I want to tell her to stay – that it's the best conversation I've had with anyone for as long as I can remember – but that sounds way too creepy. So I just stand there and watch them go.

I look back at the fountain. I wobbled hey? One last chance. I draw it in, trying to bring the energy into a spitting, spinning ball in my centre and this time, I can feel it move, just a little, and then, suddenly, I'm wet.

Landing in the fountain wasn't quite what I had

in mind but I don't care. I did it. I moved. All on my own. Knowing exactly where I was going.

I splash the water, laughing at how good it feels. And then I disappear.

CHAPTER 7

he shock of it – of zapping out again without knowing where I'm going – hits me in the chest like a fist, making me gasp with the heaviness of it. Idiot! So stupid to think that being able to do it once myself was going to stop it happening. But part of me – a big part if I'm honest – was sort of hoping that's how it'd work. And that somehow, maybe, I'd be able to return to the unit – the one with the man who gave me my name back.

I'm in a library. A big one, by the looks of it, with filtered lighting shining up the dust motes. And it's quiet. So quiet that I'm sure my gasp of air must've echoed through the aisles of books. But so far, no one's rushed over to see what I'm doing so maybe it wasn't as loud as I thought. Or maybe I'm the only one here.

I'm still wet, dripping water all over the floor,

creating a puddle already, and my shoes squelch as I walk down the end of the row. I stick my head around the shelf, looking down the central walkway. There's no one in sight. I don't know if that's a good thing or not but suddenly, I feel nervous. Like ants are crawling over my skin. Is it this place or is something else going on? I feel like I should tip-toe but that seems stupid. What have I got to fear? I wish I knew.

I swallow past the lump that's forming in my throat. I'm not a coward. At least, I don't think I am. I don't feel like I'm that sort of person and, I guess, it's what I think now that matters.

The sound of my shoes echoes through the room as I walk and I wince, wishing there was something I could do to dry off. The fabric mural hanging on the wall in a seating area on the left looks to be my best option. It has greens and browns and blues, all swirled in what honestly looks like a bit of a mess. I'm not sure what it's supposed to depict, but whatever it is, I'm not getting it. I guess I'm not into modern art either.

I send up a small thank you that no one's actually sitting there and move forward to gently coax it off the wall. I don't even tear it! I scrunch it over my body and hair, squeezing and patting as much as I can. Not the best towel but at least it manages to dry me off a little. Enough that I don't feel like a drowned rat.

I pull off my shoes too and tip the water out of them into a bin in the corner, wringing my socks out before putting them back on. It still feels terrible but it's better than squelching.

I lay the hanging over the chairs, smoothing out the wrinkles I've created, hoping it will dry a bit at least and not be totally ruined. After all, someone did take the time to make it. I hope it wasn't expensive.

I move further through the library. A few people are seated at tables at the end of the floor, books opened in front of them, absorbed in what they're reading. Only one, a man, looks up as I go by. He looks startled, probably over the fact that I'm so damp, and I run my fingers through my hair, feeling like an idiot. I meet his eyes without any feeling of connection though and continue to walk on. There are staircases in front of me – both up and down. For just a second, I'm paralysed with indecision. And then I'm heading down. Seems as good a choice as any.

There are more people on the bottom level and I only glance at them before looking away, not wanting to leave yet, despite the energy I can feel buzzing through my body.

The desk to check out the books is on my right and I move towards it like I know where I'm going. Maybe I *have* been here before. Maybe this is something else I don't know I know. Actually, there's a lot of that.

I stand at the counter, hands folded on top, waiting to be noticed by the librarian sitting at the desk. I don't know why. What the hell am I going to say to her? But my body seems to know what it's doing so I'm going to trust it. For the moment.

That's when I realise I don't actually have a book. Not that I can check one out without a name, but it'd make me more inconspicuous. There's a trolley of returned books not far from the desk and I grab the closest one to me. A mystery. Seems ironic really.

I can only see the librarian from the side. She looks to be in her early thirties and has glasses and rich, red hair curled up into a bun. What a cliché. That's all I can really see of her. Until she looks up. And then I know I know her. The energy builds in me, ready to pull me away.

I fight it, pushing hard against it, using what I learnt in the fountain, making it disperse again. I can feel myself wavering and I actually have to grit my teeth but I'm still here. Still facing the shock on the woman's face. There's no smile. Just shock.

'Oh, my God. I can't believe you're here.'

It doesn't give me much to go on but for some reason, right at this moment, I don't want to tell her the truth. Maybe because she doesn't look like she's really happy to see me. And if she's not happy to see me, it means she's not a friend. Not an enemy necessarily – not yet anyway – but not someone to trust.

'Yep. Here in the flesh.'

She gets up and comes over. I have to stop myself from taking a step away from her and feel my body waver again. It's getting harder to stay here. She stumbles against the counter and then looks at me with stunned eyes. And I know I've done it again. I felt it. I took some of her energy. Not as much as the man at the lookout – not even close, but it happened. Shit. Why can't I control this?

She puts out a hand, as if to defend herself.

'What did you do?'

I don't answer her. I just shake my head and feel my body shimmer again.

'Don't go. Please. You have to come back in.'

Back in? Back in to where? Not that I'm going to ask and give myself away. I square my shoulders.

'Why should I? What if I don't want to?'

She blanches, like she's afraid of me. Or of someone else. My heart's thumping and I know that I'm not going to be able to stop the energy from zapping me away for much longer. She reaches down behind the counter and I'm imagining all types of things – a gun, a panic alarm – but all she does is bring up a business card.

'Please. Charles said that if anyone sees you, we're to tell you to ring him. He said to say that it can all be sorted out.'

I nod, like I know exactly what she's talking about. Faking it. Because I'm trying desperately not to show what the name Charles is doing to me. How it's making my stomach roll and squeeze in on itself, twisting into knots. How it's making my thoughts race in panic like a herd of stampeding cattle.

I reach out for the card, even though I don't want it. Not if just the name makes me feel this bad. But it will hopefully give me answers and I definitely need those. I'm ridiculously pleased that my hands are only slightly trembling.

'Why don't you just go to him? Why do you need to ring?' She looks like she's feeling braver. I don't like it. I don't like it and I don't like her.

'None of your business.'

'If you want, I can ring him for you. Now.'

She seems far too eager to do that and I shake my head. She looks disappointed and for some reason, that makes me feel good.

'Don't forget to tell him that it was me who gave you the card.'

I just nod.

I've got no intention of telling her that I don't have a clue who she is. Not that I have the time anyway. With the card in my hand, I can't hold it back anymore.

I am gone.

CHAPTER 8

I don't have to gasp for air this time. It's smoother, easier. Like my body's getting used to the movement.

I'm in a shopping centre. Sunshine Central Plaza, it says above the information desk, which tells me nothing. It's teaming with people going about their business and the noise of it after the quiet of the library is almost overwhelming. Not that it matters. The important thing is I still have the card in my hand.

I take the time to look at it now.

Charles Clarke. Managing Director of a company called RACE. And a phone number. That's it. I flip the card over but it's blank. Just a perfect white rectangle that tells me absolutely nothing about who Charles Clarke is or what RACE actually does. No clue as to why he wants me to ring him…why he wants me to come back in, whatever that means.

It takes all of my self-control not to just throw it in the bin and again, it makes me wonder what the hell has happened to me. Maybe I *should* just throw it away – start a whole new life – except it's hard to start a new life when there's still so much about myself I don't know. Jesus, I still don't even know what my last name is! Or why I can do this energy thing. Or how to control it. Or what the man in the bed means to me…

And I've got no money. Well, twenty dollars that I found stuffed in my shorts' pocket when I put the photo there. Not really conducive to starting again.

No, if I want to be able to move on, I need to know what I'm leaving behind first.

There's a sign for public phones and I follow it down a small alleyway in the centre. It's only when I pick up the receiver that I realise I don't have either coins or a card to make it work. I roll my eyes and lean my forehead against the cold metal of the console. Can nothing be easy? Just once?

'Are you okay? Can I help you with anything?'

I look up. There's a woman standing next to me – no zapping so I obviously don't know her. She looks…normal. Dark hair, greying at the sides, three quarter length pants, modest top with beads around the top…normal.

'Sorry?'

'You look upset. I was just wondering if there was anything I could do to help.'

I shake my head, my brain buzzing with possibilities of why she might be talking to me. Is she connected to Charles? Does she know him? Is she linked with RACE, whatever that is? But that can't be right, otherwise I'd recognise her. Paranoid. God, I'm messed up. What was my life like before?

'I just need change for the phone. But I'll go into one of the stores and get it.'

She reaches into her wallet and presses some coins into my hand. I want to give them straight back, which is stupid. It's just change, for God's sake! But it means more than that. It means we're tied somehow. Connected, even in this small way. She's smiling at me. I don't smile back.

'Think about it as my good deed for the day.'

'Thanks, but I have money.'

She's still smiling but it's like she's not listening to me. And she doesn't take back the money I'm holding out to her either. She just pats my hand.

'The shops don't usually like to give change for the phone. Please, take the money. You remind me of my granddaughter. She'd be about your age – about twenty?'

I nod, even though I have no idea how old I am.

She reaches out to touch my hair. 'Besides which, it looks like you need someone to take care of you for a little while.'

I don't know what to say to that. But I can feel tears prickling in my eyes like some sort of sentimental school girl and blink to make them go away. She's probably right. Not that I need someone to take care of me – I don't – but I probably need a shower and a hairbrush. Any sort of personal care has been lost in the fact that I've been trying to find out about the inner me. The physical me has just had to wait.

I grip the money in my fist, feeling the metal dig into my skin. Why is it so hard to accept her help? What does that say about me? But I don't feel like I can give it back now without being a total and utter bitch. And she doesn't deserve that. She's just trying to be nice. Caring. So I nod.

'Thank you.' It feels stilted but still, I've said it.

She pats my arm, just once, and leaves me to make the call. Part of me wants to ask her to come back. Wait with me so I'm not alone. I must be in a bad way to want the company of just anyone – a total stranger. I take a deep breath. I need to keep it together.

Before I can chicken out, I push the coins into the slot and wait for the dial tone. The buzz in my ear to tell me it's working should be comforting. But it's not. I push the hand set harder against the side of my head, feeling the cold metal against my skin and push the phone number in like the buttons have personally insulted me.

It seems to ring forever before there's a click on the other end.

'Yes.'

It's a male. A voice I've heard before even if I can't picture the face that goes with it. A voice that makes me break into a cold sweat. I can't talk. I should just hang up but I'm frozen – paralysed with…fear? Who is he? Is it this Charles or someone else? And what has he done in my past that gets this reaction from me when I can't even remember who he is? Jesus!

'Who is this?'

He sounds angry now, like I'm wasting his time, but I still can't find any words. I can feel the energy in me though, surging, trying to pull me away. My control is getting better.

'Rhiannon?'

I jerk the phone away like it's about to bite me and slam the receiver back in its hook. How did he know? Pure guess? I don't know what connection I have with him but whatever instinctual reactions I still have obviously aren't okay with this. My breathing is back to gasping and I have to lean against the phone to try and stop the nausea that's threatening to come up. I focus on the coolness of the metal on my forehead, trying to get control.

A control I almost lose again when the phone rings. The shock of it is enough to make me stumble back and I only just manage not to fall over. I stare at it, panic racing through me, urging me to run. All I can think is that he's found me. He knows where I am. Fuck!

I don't know how I'm brave – or stupid – enough to pick up the phone but I do.

CHAPTER 9

'Hello.'

It isn't him. It's a female voice.

'Rhiannon?'

'Who is this?'

'It's Macy. I saw you in the café yesterday. Before you…left.'

Macy. It's vaguely familiar. And she isn't freaking out about the fact that I disappeared into thin air – well I'm assuming that's what it looked like anyway – so she must know something about all of this. Like the boy in the bed…

'Are you still there?'

'Yes.'

'Charles asked me to call this number back. He's worried about you. He wants you to come in. Let us help you.'

'Why?'

That seems to throw her, like she didn't think I'd ask questions. She must be stupid. Or maybe she doesn't know me very well. Then again, maybe I've changed. Anything's possible.

'Well, he's worried about you.'

'Why is he worried?'

There's a pause so long I wonder if she's actually hung up on me. And then I wonder if he's there. Listening. Telling her what to say.

'Charles knows you don't remember much…'

I can't work out if she's asking me a question or if she actually knows what's happening for me. It feels like a bluff.

'He knows shit.'

There's another pause. And then he's on the line. I knew it! I knew he was there. But even being right doesn't make me feel good.

'Rhiannon, enough. I'm going to send Macy to get you. You are to come back in and let us help you. Stay where you are. She'll be there shortly.'

I can hear his breathing on the phone – rapid like he's run a race. So he's reacting to this call too. That's interesting. Not interesting enough that I'm going to answer him though. Which must be really pissing him off because I can hear it in his voice.

'Just stay there. Do you understand? Do what I tell you.'

And then he hangs up. Just like that. Like he doesn't care what I think. Like he's expecting me to do what I'm told. I almost snort. I would if I didn't feel so scared. What is it about him that causes this reaction in me?

I want to run away. Or zap away at least. I'm only just keeping that in check. Because as much as I want to go, this is the perfect opportunity to find out more. Who are they? What do they do? How am I connected to them? And where do they want to take me?

If I could follow Macy back to wherever they are, maybe that would bring some memories back. Or maybe I'd even have the opportunity to do some digging – find things – like I did at my mum's house.

The shop across from the telephones is packed with cheap clothes. Perfect for what I need. I grab a hat, a thin, cotton scarf in blues and white and a vest to go over my shirt. It's a sort of disguise anyway. Enough that, if I'm careful, she won't notice me. Not straight away at least. It's the best I can do at such short notice. It takes almost thirteen of my twenty dollars and it's a wrench to have to hand it over but worth it. Hopefully.

I stand just inside the shop, pretending that I'm looking at other clothes as I wait for her to come. It's only ten minutes after the phone call when she hurries in, head flicking from side to side like she's looking for something. Or someone. Me. I have to resist the urge to duck down.

Her blonde hair is in a ponytail and it's swinging

like it's got a life of its own. I don't know why I notice that but I need to get it together – focus. She stops at the phones and touches one like it's going to tell her where I am. And then she turns in a slow circle, looking. Her eyes don't really rest on me at all. But then, to be fair, I'm barely taller than the clothes rack so she can't really see much of me except the hat. One time when being short is an advantage.

That thought stops me. Don't I like being short? I close my eyes for a second, poking that idea, turning it over, examining it. No, I don't. I don't like being short! Huh, well there you go.

When I open my eyes again, Macy has already started to move off. Crap! Keep up brain! I wait until she's almost out of the glass doors before I follow her. In a lime green, flowy shirt, she's not going to be hard to miss. Not that she should wear that colour – it makes her look sallow. Huh, maybe I'm a bit of a bitch as well.

I'm amazed how quickly she can walk in high heels – the woman's like a machine, for God's sake – and have to hurry to keep up with her as she dodges people on the sidewalk like she's done this all her life. Maybe she has.

And then, she stops and turns.

My heart catapults into my throat and I have to pull the energy back as it tries to zap me away. It feels like I flicker, like it did in the park, and I'm praying that she doesn't see me – mentally crossing everything I can. I have to push myself to keep walking, to not react, because that will only draw attention to me. It's hard to pretend that her standing there, eyes moving, moving, searching – searching for *me* – doesn't concern me.

It's only when her face falls in disappointment and she turns back around that I can breathe again. She's not as stupid as she looks then, trying to catch me out like that. I wonder what Charles will say though when she goes back in and tells him that she couldn't find me. I wouldn't want to be in her shoes, and not just because they're high heels.

She darts from the gutter side of the sidewalk to the row of glass buildings that loom over us. So fast that I almost lose her. What is with this woman? Is she a frigging spy or something? She stops for a moment to press a button on the green glass door of the building in front of her but I'm too far away to see what it is. And then the door is opening and she's going through. I hurry to catch up, not really sure what I'm going to do – even to catch a glimpse inside would be good – but it closes before I get there.

I dare a quick glance at the door as I go by. The button she pressed is for a speaker system, meaning I'd have to identify myself in order to gain entry. And there's no way that's happening.

The only other thing on the door is the symbol for RACE – a stylised image of Earth with the initials stamped over it – big, bold, making no attempt at humility. Tells you everything and nothing all at the same time. And yet, my steps falter for a moment when I see it. Because I've seen that sign before.

I know it.

And I hate it.

My mouth is suddenly dry and I have to resist the urge to run, get away, make myself safe. Shit! I try to walk normally, pulling back on the energy that really, *really* wants to get me out of there. It's the hardest thing I've ever done. Well, that I can remember anyway.

I'm so busy focusing on breathing and walking and not zapping away that I almost walk past the person sitting on the bench a few buildings up. It's not until my eyes lock with his that I realise it's the man from the bed.

And that he's looking at me.

CHAPTER 10

The shock of seeing him pulls me up short, and I stop, staring, before my brain can decide whether it's a smart thing to do or not. I'm warring with the energy that's trying its hardest to take me away, like a little kid at its mother's skirt, tugging and pulling, wanting attention. It's difficult to concentrate on both – on the energy and on him – but my control is getting better. I don't even waver this time.

His shock seems to equal mine. He recovers quicker than me though. Suddenly he's on his feet, wrapping me in his arms. And all my stupid brain can think is how good he smells. Not just the aftershave he's wearing but him. *He* smells good.

'Christ, Rhi,' he says. 'You just left. I didn't know if I'd ever see you again! We can talk about this. Please.'

I have no idea what we have to talk about but I don't say that. I don't say anything. I'm too stunned that he's actually here and that I'm in his arms and that I still want him as much as I did this morning. I want to wrap my arms around him and rest my head on his chest and see if his heart is beating as fast as mine. But I can't. I want to but I don't know him. He's not any less of a stranger than when I wanted to climb into bed with him.

It only takes him a moment to realise I'm not responding and he leans back out of the hug, his hands going around my upper arms. He looks sad and I have to fight the need to touch his face, comfort him, soothe him.

'Please Rhi, don't do this. Can't we just talk?'

I take a deep breath, trying to be brave. Because his reaction to what I'm about to ask seems important. Although I'm not sure why.

'Listen, don't take this the wrong way, but who are you?'

The creases in his forehead get deeper and I want to smooth them out with my finger but I stay still, looking at him. Waiting. Praying. Hoping. Even if I don't know what I'm hoping for.

'What?'

I look away from his eyes – his beautiful blue eyes that I could absolutely get lost in – and down at my shoes.

'Well, you obviously…know me. You know my

name, know things about me.' I look back up. 'But I don't have any idea who you are. Don't feel bad though, I don't even know who I am.'

I attempt a smile but it doesn't work. Not when I'm faced with the obvious confusion on his face.

How is it that I can tell him all this when I was so desperate to keep it from Charles? Tell him all this when I don't even know if I can trust him? And yet, I'm not getting the same reaction to him as I did to Charles. Well, I'm getting the same butterflies in the stomach and pounding heart but I'm pretty sure they're for totally different reasons…

He lets his hands fall from my arms and as soon as they're gone, I want them back. I want his touch, his hands on me. Or his lips… My chest tightens at the thought. I must be screwed up. How can I want him this badly and yet not remember him?

'Are you joking?'

I shake my head, wishing that I didn't care so much about his reaction. Wishing I could just walk away now. Walk away and protect myself when all I want to do is stay. I push my hair back, trying for nonchalance, trying not to let him see my desperation. Pretending a strength I don't feel.

'Why? Would I normally joke about something this serious?'

He cocks his head to look at me.

'Yeah, actually you would.'

There you go – I must be a bitch. A bitch or a smart arse anyway.

'Well you'll just have to take my word for it. It's all gone. The only reason I know my first name is because you told me this morning when you were… asleep. In bed. In your bedroom.'

I rush the words out and can feel the blush on my skin, the tightening of my stomach muscles at the thought of his chest and his stomach and whatever the sheet was covering. He doesn't seem to notice, thank God! Or maybe he's just being polite. He shakes his head.

'Christ, I can't believe this. Come on, let's go somewhere and we'll talk.'

He takes my hand and I follow, like a little puppy, even though my brain's telling me I should stand up for myself – demand that he tells me everything before I go anywhere with him. I ignore it. For the moment, it's nice to not have to think and to just surrender to someone who looks like they know what's going on.

I must be an idiot as well as a bitch.

CHAPTER 11

He takes me to a coffee shop on the corner. It's been done up retro style. All red, white, silver and black with records on the wall and padded booths to sit in. I love it straight away and slip behind one of the tables, one at the back in the corner, waiting for…I still don't know his name, how weird is that…to join me. He gives me a look – one that tells me that maybe he doesn't believe me.

'What?'

'This is your favourite table. You choose this one every time we come here.'

I don't know what to say to that so I don't say anything. I just stare him out and finally he sighs and looks down at the table.

'What *do* you remember?'

'Initially, not much. Vague feelings about being

places. Like I said, you told me what my name was. And I think I found my home. Or my mum's anyway. And I sort of remember, from looking at photos, that I have a brother?'

His head jerks up at this and my heart trips over itself at his reaction. The feeling that I had at my mother's house – that desperate worry - rushes back, engulfing me in a single wave that threatens to drown me.

'What's wrong? Is he okay?'

He frowns again and shakes his head. But this time, he doesn't look at me.

'Nothing. Nothing's wrong.'

I don't believe him. But I need information. Any information. And if he won't start here – if for some reason, he doesn't want to tell me about my brother – I'll start somewhere else. And then we'll come back to this. Because I won't be able to keep a lid on this feeling of panic for too long.

'So, who are you?'

It comes out harsher than I expected – some of the fear leaking out despite my best efforts.

'I'm Josh. Josh Dixon.'

His name stirs something in me; something deep down in my gut, making everything tighten. I try to ignore it.

'And Josh – Josh Dixon – how do you know me?'

He stares at me again and I have to blink to not be drawn in.

'You really don't remember, do you?'

'I can't believe you still think I'm joking. Why would I do that? Christ! I don't remember, okay?'

I just want him to tell me. Tell me everything. Talk until his voice is hoarse. Now. Before something else happens and I don't get the chance and I'm lost again.

'We were engaged. I was your fiancé.'

He says it deadpanned. Emotionlessness. Like we're talking about something inane. The weather. Or the coffee at the shop. Not about the fact that we were obviously in love; that I knew this man well enough to want to marry him. That he wanted to marry me back. How can I not remember that?

'Fuck!'

'Well, thanks. That's the response I was looking for.'

He sounds pissed now, which is so not my fault. Engaged! God, it feels surreal. Like I'm in a dream. How can this be my life when I don't remember any of it? How can I trust anything when I don't know if it's true? I look down at my hand.

'Why aren't I wearing a ring?'

He squirms, like I've caught him out, and looks down at his own hands, clasped on the table in front of him. He has long fingers. Nice hands. Which is not something I need to be focusing on.

'You broke it off four days ago. The day before you disappeared.'

I sit back, a sick feeling swirling in my stomach, watching him, trying to work out what this means, how I feel about it. Trying to digest all of this new information when none of it makes any sense.

'Why did I break it off?'

He laughs. It sounds like I've mortally wounded him.

'Christ, are you kidding me? I don't know why you called it off! We were good. I thought we were at least. You just turned up at my place and told me you weren't ready to commit. Whatever that frigging means.'

I feel like the me I was before all this – the one I only have vague memories of – was a real bitch. Or maybe I was just strong – a woman who knew her own mind. If only that was still true!

His hand is only centimetres from mine on the table…almost touching. So close that all I'd have to do is move my fingers and I'd be touching his skin, running my fingertips over his knuckles, bringing his hand up to my mouth, the tip of one finger between my lips…

I shake my head. Jesus. What's wrong with me?

'Were we in love?' I blurt the words out before I get the chance to think about them and then wish I hadn't. I want to stuff them back into my mouth - leave them unsaid - but there's part of me that wants to know the answer too.

He holds my gaze, like he's trying to work out what I'm thinking. Like I'm confusing him.

'Yes.' It's soft. Caressing.

'Oh.'

He slides out from behind the table, standing up beside me. I watch him, frozen, waiting to see what he's going to do, nervous all of a sudden. I can feel the energy pulling at me, trying to make me safe. But I'm not sure how I *can* be safe from him. Not when I react to him like I do.

'Can we try something?'

'What?'

'Don't question Rhi, just trust.'

It's hard. Every instinct is telling me to back away. Don't trust. Keep yourself safe. And yet, I must have trusted him at some stage. Trusted him enough to say yes to a proposal, anyway. But then I broke it off too. And maybe it was over something he did. Something I found out. Maybe he cheated on me!

He's staring at me, waiting, his eyebrows raised like he thinks I'll chicken out. I don't know if it's the challenge he's silently giving me or the fact that he called me Rhi, but I give a half-hearted shrug that covers the fact that all my organs are tying themselves in knots.

'Whatever.'

'Stand up.'

I do and he moves back a little to give me room.

I look up at him. He must be over six foot. And then he takes a step in, closer to me, and I forget to breathe. He wraps his hand around the side of my head, his thumb next to my ear, the rest of his fingers caressing the skin of my neck. Cradling me. I want to lean into his touch but I don't. I hold myself stiff, waiting, despite the fact that heat is racing under my skin, through my body, making everything pull tight.

He brings his head down, closer. So close that I can feel his breath on my skin. He stops and I can see the different shades of blue around his pupil as he looks at me. I'm drowning in the desire I can see in his face and shut my eyes, overwhelmed by my own need for him. He makes a low groaning sound and the vibration feels like it travels through me, aligning us, and then his lips are on mine. They are soft, gentle. Small kisses, filled with sighs, where he pulls back slightly between each one. Teasing me until I can't stand it.

My hand goes around the back of his neck as if it has a life of its own and I pull him harder against me.

And then he's kissing me. Really kissing. He sucks on my upper lip and a moan escapes me before I can stop it. He pulls me closer, his other hand around my back under my shirt, tracing the bottom half of my spine, distracting me, driving me crazy, making me forget what he's told me. I jump up at him, needing to be closer, wrapping my legs around his waist so that we're the same height. He holds me easily as our kisses become deeper, harder, his tongue driving me crazy in a way that drives out all rational thought.

I don't know how long we kiss before we pull back, our breathing loud and ragged. He laughs then – a nice one that sends shivers down my spine. And then I remember that I don't know if I can trust him. No matter how good he looks or how nice he smells or how great he kisses…or how much I want to keep kissing him, all over his body…I don't know him.

Jesus! Was I a nymphomaniac as well in my forgotten life? One look from this guy and I'm ready to jump his bones! And in a public place, for God's sake! If I didn't have information to get from him, I'd leave now. Run away. Probably…

He's smiling at me. 'Christ, I've missed you. I love you.'

The energy tugs at me again – get out, get away! It's harder to control this time and I suck in a breath, trying to make it respond to me. He frowns at me, not angry I don't think, but questioning. Maybe over the fact that I haven't said I love you back. Not that there's any chance he's getting that. I'm in deep enough already. Time to detach.

He puts me down and it's suddenly awkward, like a first kiss gone wrong. He's still holding my hand

and I pull away, tugging at my clothes, adjusting the stupid vest that I'd wish I'd taken off before I'd seen him. Even though there's a part of me that doesn't want to pull away. A part of me that, for the first time since this all started, doesn't feel alone. I tell that part to shut up as we sit down again.

I clear my throat. 'So, tell me a bit about myself.'

'What do you want to know first?' His voice is neutral again. I don't know if I've hurt his feelings or if he's trying not to overwhelm me. Which would make him a nice guy – someone I could trust. This is so hard. So bloody confusing!

'Well, a full name would be nice.'

'Rhiannon Thyme Clarke.'

I screw up my face. 'Thyme? What, as in tick tock?'

He laughs. 'No, as in the herb. You've always hated it. I think it was your Mum who chose it.'

And then the last name hits me and I hold myself still, feeling the energy whip around my body like a cyclone on steroids.

'Clarke?'

Josh goes still too.

'Yep.'

'As in Charles Clarke?'

He nods, watching me, the wariness back in his eyes.

'He's your Dad, Rhi.'

I feel the energy pulling me away. It's too big, I can't contain it. I don't know how to this time.

'Josh!'

'Hold on to me! Don't let go.'

I take his hand, gripping it, digging fingernails in. And then I'm gone.

CHAPTER 12

I am back at the unit…Josh's unit. It looks different in the daylight. And I'm still holding his hand. He is here with me, leaning over, sucking in air like he doesn't think he'll ever be able to breathe again.

I kneel down on the carpet, thoughts in a whirl, waiting for him to recover and give me answers.

'What happened?'

'I directed us here.'

'You directed us?'

He nods. 'I can stream too.'

The name clicks into place somewhere in my brain. Streaming. I'm a streamer. And so is Josh.

'I can't control it very well. I don't remember how. Could I ever do it? Direct it like you can?'

He kneels beside me, wrapping his arm around my shoulders and pulling me in closer. I let him do it. I'm not sure why but at the moment, it seems easier than pulling back. That's what I tell myself anyway.

'You're one of the best streamers.'

I can hear something in his voice.

'What's the but?'

'Nothing. There's no but. Losing your memory has obviously taken away your control.'

I don't believe him but I'm okay to leave it for the moment. There are too many other questions to ask.

'Can you teach me to control it again?'

'Of course.'

I want to snuggle in closer, to really revel in the feel of his arms around me. So, I hold myself stiff in his arms instead. I need to keep focused. Answers. That's what I need. Not this…physical response to him. I'm worried that if I give into it, I might never find myself. I will be happy to be lost…happy to trust him, even if I shouldn't.

It's then that I realise how tired I am. For the first time in four days, I desperately want to sleep. Not from emotional exhaustion but from physical exhaustion.

And then I remember the man. The one at the lookout. The one I killed. The one I've been able to forget about for a while, like it meant nothing.

I pull back from Josh's embrace. He doesn't say anything, just lets me go, watching me. My mouth is dry and I run my tongue over my teeth, trying to find the words. I have to tell him – well, I have to tell someone, so it might as well be him.

'I killed someone.'

'What?' His eyebrows are shooting up his forehead. Maybe I shouldn't have said it as bluntly as that – like a slap to the head. But I don't know how else to say it. It's not like it's something that slips easily into conversation.

'I killed someone. A guy. He was trying to…well, he was trying to rape me. And somehow, I don't know how, I sort of…sucked all the energy out of him. That's what it felt like anyway. I didn't mean to. But I'm pretty sure he was dead when I zapped out. Streamed.'

He pulls me in again and I can feel his chin on the top of my head.

'Jesus, Rhi. I can't believe what you've been through. Christ!'

I'm waiting for the judgement – for him to tell me that I'm a terrible person but it doesn't come. He just continues to hug me, hand moving over my back in a comforting rhythm.

'I didn't tell anyone about him. I didn't even know where I was to be able to let them know.'

I can feel him shake his head.

'It doesn't matter. All that matters is you're safe.'

I take a deep breath, trying to get the courage to ask the question that's been sitting in my brain, like an infection, waiting to spread its horrors.

'Is that something we can do as streamers? Are we bad people?'

The movement of his hand stops for a moment but then starts again, slightly harder, as if he's trying to prove something.

'You're not bad, Rhi. He was trying to rape you! You must have been so scared. You have to believe me, I was trying to find you. Trying to work out where you were so we could talk. For four days, I've been crazy with worry about what was happening to you, where you were, what you were doing, if you were okay, thinking you'd just decided to take off. No word of where you were going or when you'd be back. And you didn't take any of your stuff.' There's silence for a moment. 'Do you know what happened? How you lost your memory?'

I shake my head. 'All I remember is streaming one place to the next, not knowing how it worked or what was happening. Not knowing anything.'

'Christ! I'm so sorry.'

'It's not your fault.' At least, I don't think it is. But it could be. Maybe he was the last person I saw before all this started happening…when I broke it off with him. Even though he says it was the next day I disappeared. My brain hurts with all the unknowns. I just want to not think! I try to stifle a yawn but it doesn't work.

'I don't want that to keep happening – the streaming. I can't live like that. You have to teach me…' My eyes are shutting and I let them go. 'I need you to teach me how to do it. To stream properly again.'

'Don't worry. You're safe now.' His voice sounds really faint but I know he's still there, watching over me. And as I drift off to sleep, for the first time in what feels like ages, I'm not worried. Shows you how stupid I can be.

CHAPTER 13

I wake with a start, heart pounding. For a moment, I don't know where I am. And then I see brown and know I'm lying on Josh's couch with a blanket pulled over the top of me and the unit is starting to darken in the late afternoon light.

'Josh!'

I don't like the panic in my voice.

'Hey, it's okay. I'm here.'

He comes out of the bedroom, shorts on but shirt in his hand. His hair is wet. 'Are you okay?'

I run my hand over my eyes. 'I must have had a nightmare.'

But I don't think it's that. For that split second of waking, all I could think was that I'd streamed again before Josh could tell me how to control it. I don't like being scared. I sit up, swinging my legs off of the lounge, and fold the blanket up on my lap. Order. Control. That's what I need.

'How's your energy?'

I frown, trying to feel for it.

'Low still.'

'You need to have something to eat.'

I watch him go into the small kitchen, separated from the lounge only by the bench that juts out from the wall. The muscles in his back ripple as he moves to get things out of the higher cupboards. God, he is gorgeous.

'This will be the first time I've had something to eat in days. Since I lost my memory anyway.'

He goes still, arms up in the cupboard. It's only for a second but it's enough to let me know that what I've said isn't normal. Even for streamers. It feels like the same pause he had last night when I told me about the dead man. The pause that says I'm strange…what I'm doing is weird. I lean forward, heart skipping a beat for a whole different reason now.

'What's wrong?'

He shakes his head and turns around to put things on the bench but he's not looking at me.

'Nothing. It's all good. You just need some food.' His voice sounds like he's trying to force it to be normal. It makes me feel worse. Like I can't get anything right. Not the streaming or my memory or this thing I had with him…the relationship.

I get up, putting the blanket on the edge of the lounge, fixing it so it's tidy, and walk over, sitting on the stool that had been pushed under the bench. Josh is still not looking at me and I put my hand over his, stopping his movements.

'I'm not stupid. I know this isn't right. You have to tell me what's going on. Please.'

He shuts his eyes for a moment, taking his hand away and running it through his hair. When he looks at me again, I can see worry there. Worry for me. Shit. He looks at me, saying nothing, and I just look back. It's hard to stay quiet. I just want to argue the point, tell him he has no choice, that he has to tell me, that I deserve to know, to just get it over with, for God's sake! But it seems smarter just to shut up. I have to bite on the edge of my tongue though. Finally, he nods.

'Alright, I'll tell you, but eat something first.'

He pushes a banana towards me and I screw up my nose. He smiles.

'I know you don't like them but it'll give you the quickest energy boost.'

I pick it up, holding it in front of me.

'I don't like them?'

He shakes his head but takes it off me and half peels it anyway. I hesitate and he grins at me.

'Come on, don't be a baby. Eat this and I'll tell you everything I know.'

I scowl at him but grab it and take the biggest

bite I can. It's mushy and thick and horrible in my mouth and I have to concentrate on chewing and swallowing. Three bites and it's gone. I slam the skin on the bench.

'There. Happy? Now, tell me.'

He puts his hand on mine, running his thumb over my inner wrist. It does wonderful things to my insides, warping them, tying them in knots. My breath catches in my throat. His eyes are darker when he looks at me. I should pull away. I should…

'You know, I love it when you get bossy.'

I have to swallow in order to talk and my voice is husky when it comes out.

'Stop trying to distract me.'

He laughs and it does the same thing as his touch. I just want to leap over the bench and run my hands down his chest, feel his skin under mine. I want to lick the little droplets of water left over from the shower from his body. I want him to groan for me. I'm standing up before I even realise I'm doing it. And he's watching me with a hunger that's nearly my undoing.

I shake my head, closing my eyes as if that's going to stop my body's response to him. When I open them again, he's standing in front of me. There's no question that he wants me as much as I want him. This gorgeous guy wants me. Me! I'm under no illusions about my appearance. When I looked in the mirror, I saw a moderately cute girl staring back –

short dark hair, grey-green eyes, tiny. Not stunning or beautiful or even particularly interesting. Cute. That's it. How could he want me?

And why the hell did I break up with him? Someone this hot and charming and seemingly nice. He must have done something terrible for me to end it. Not that any of that seems really important at the moment…

He leans down and I think he's going for my lips, but he changes direction and is kissing my neck, making his way from my ear to my collar bone. His hand slips up under my shirt and traces up my side, from the curve of my waist to just underneath my breast. My breath catches, trapped by the hunger that's swelling up in me – the thought of leaning into him, guiding his hand up to my swollen nipple, already craving the touch of his hand, his lips. I want more.

Each touch feels like it's lighting fireworks inside my body, the wick sizzling on its way to explosion, until I'm not sure that I can stand anymore without giving in to him. And I can't give in. I can't afford to. I need information. I need to learn how to control the shifting…just in case I disappear again.

I grab his hair and pull his head up. He lets me do it.

'We need to stop.' My breathless voice doesn't sound as assertive as I want it to. He grins and kisses me, one long, hard kiss where he molds my body to his with his touch and I can feel how much he wants me. And then he pulls back. I actually stagger a bit when he loosens his hold.

'Okay, I'm stopping.'

I know this is what I've asked for but I'm not sure it's really what I want. It's on the tip of my lips to ask him to touch me again but I shake my head. Later. There'll be time later to re-explore the things I've forgotten. Time to work out what happened between the two of us.

I re-arrange my clothes, taking the time to get my thinking back in order rather than feeling like it's being ravaged by hormones. Taking the time to get my breathing back to normal. It's hard. With my back to the bench, I jump up so that I'm sitting on it, legs dangling. Josh sits on the stool I was sitting on before, his arm draped over my legs. It'd probably be better if he wasn't touching me at all but my hormone-driven side is willing to take it as a poor second, so I shut up to keep it happy.

'Okay, spill it. I want to know everything. You promised.'

He sighs.

'Right, well you know about RACE.'

'I only know its name. That's all. From a card I was given by a librarian?'

He nods. 'Carly. She's one of our contacts. The library is an important meeting point. Charles has had everyone looking out for you.'

That doesn't make me feel any better.

'Tell me about Charles.'

'What do you want to know?' There's a hesitation to his voice.

'I don't know. What's he like? Is he a good person?'

He frowns at me. 'Why would you ask me that?'

I shrug, looking away from him. 'No reason.'

'Rhi.'

I sigh. 'Every time I see his name or hear his voice, I freak out. I don't know why, I just do. Why is that? If he's my dad...'

I want to know the answer to this one so badly I hold my breath waiting for him to talk. Because if I know this, then I can make sure it doesn't keep on happening. I can control it. Maybe.

'Christ Rhi, I don't know. I mean, you've never been close to your Dad. But I don't think you've ever been scared of him.' I wait for something else. I can sense the 'but' in his voice. He shakes his head. 'He has been…different the last few months.'

'Different how?'

'I don't know. More…intense. He's a hard man to please. And he doesn't have a lot of time for feelings. His or anyone else's. And he's ambitious. Like, really ambitious.'

I don't like the picture I'm getting. How can I be related to this man? Shit!

'What does RACE stand for?'

'It stands for Rhiannon, Adam, Charles enterprises.' He pauses, like he's waiting for something and I know what it is. I grip my hands tight in front of me, bones pressing together.

'Adam. That's my brother, isn't it?'

He nods, waiting still. The stirring of uneasiness that I got before – the feeling that something isn't right; really not right – is fighting its way up from my stomach, choking me.

'What's happened to him? Where is he?'

Josh frowns.

'Why do you think something's happened?'

I put my hand down and lean forward slightly.

'I don't know. I just…get this feeling. Like there's something I need to be worried about with him. Like there's something I need to do. Now.'

Josh shakes his head. 'No-one's even really sure where he is.'

'So he's disappeared, just like I did?'

'Well, yeah, I guess. Sort of. But Charles isn't looking for him like he was for you so he mustn't be worried. No one's seen him for a while though.'

I don't know what to make of that. Should I be worried then? Or are all of these stupid feelings of anxiety whenever I think of Adam just something made up in my head? I want to get up and pace – make the energy that's coursing through me go somewhere else – but I don't want to move either. I close my eyes, focusing on it, calming it down like a wild animal being tamed. When I open them again, Josh is holding on to the bench with one hand, like he's holding himself down.

'Control it, Rhi. Make it do what you want.'

I glare at him.

'What do you think I'm trying to do? Don't just tell me to control it. Tell me how.'

His hand grips my leg just above my knee. I can feel his fingers pressing into my skin.

'Think about the energy like a living thing. Every time you get emotional, it's going to respond to that. You need to breath, focus on where it's going. You used to say that for you, it felt like a lava flow.'

He's right. That's what it feels like. And now that I stop to think about it, it does respond to how I'm feeling, like a volcano waiting to explode. I take a deep breath, letting it fill my lungs, holding it and then letting it out slowly. It's only when I do it a second and a third time that I start to feel like I've got it under control.

I nod at Josh but he's already taken his hand away from my leg.

'I'm okay.'

He nods back at me but he looks tired.

'Are you?'

He rubs his hand across his eyes 'Am I what?'

'Okay.'

'Sure.'

I don't believe him. There's something in his voice – something flat.

'Bullshit.'

'Don't Rhi. Leave it. You've just calmed down.'

'You said you'd tell me everything.'

He shakes his head at the ceiling, like he's wondering how he ended up in this place with me, before standing and pacing in front of me, hands clasped together on top of his head. I sit still, watching him go back and forth, trying to be patient. Trying to keep calm, even though my breathing has sped up again. It's hard.

'There's stuff that's happened that I don't really understand. Your Dad…'

He stops and puts his hands on his hips, staring down at the floor.

'My Dad what?'

He looks at me. 'Did you realize, just then, that you were pulling energy from me?'

I grip the front of the bench, frozen, thoughts back to the lookout…to the man on the bench with dead eyes…The one I killed by taking his energy. But that can't be right. I can't be doing the same thing. He must be talking about something else. He has to be.

CHAPTER 14

'What do you mean?'

'When we stream, we use a small fraction of the energy around us – from people, animals, plants – whatever's around. Just enough to go where we want. Never enough that they'd really notice. You were sucking it out of me, Rhi. Draining me.'

I'm shaking my head before he's even finished talking. No. That can't be right. The guy at the lookout – that was an accident. It only happened because of what he was trying to do. I wouldn't do that to Josh. Except that I feel good. Energised. And I'm pretty sure it's not the effects of the stupid banana.

He must see the expression on my face because he goes to move towards me. I scoot back on the bench and hold my hands up.

'Don't! Don't come near me.'

He stops.

'It's okay. You've got it under control.'

I shake my head, tears starting to form in my eyes. Jesus. What am I?

'Did I always do that? Drain energy like that?'

There's a pause. A pause that means no. But he shakes his head just to confirm it.

'What's happened to me? What am I?'

'You're Rhi. Rhiannon. That's all that matters.'

There is more to say – I'm sure of it. More than he knows.

'Bullshit. I killed a man. How can that happen without me knowing what I'm doing?'

He goes to open his mouth but a sharp rap on the front door of his unit stops him. Adrenalin floods my body, even though I have no idea who it could be. Crazy. Josh grips my hand.

'Don't let the energy take you, okay?'

I lick my lips.

'I'll try.'

He nods and then points towards the bedroom.

'Go in there. Close the door.'

'Do you think it's Charles?'

'Maybe.'

'Don't tell them I'm here.'

I can hear that note of desperation in my voice again. I don't like it but I can't seem to stop it.

'Of course not.'

The look he gives me tells me to trust him. But I still don't know that I can. Lusting after is a whole lot different to trusting.

The knock comes again and I scoot off the bench and run to the bedroom, leaving the door open just a crack. Enough that I'll be able to listen.

I hear Josh open the door.

'Charles, hi. What's up?'

Charles! God! I know I asked but I didn't think it would really be him. The energy surges, wanting to get me out. I feel like I'm fighting with a greased pig – I try to grab at it to control it but it keeps slipping out of my grasp. I close my eyes, trying harder. It works well enough that I'm still here.

'Joshua. Have you seen Rhiannon?'

'No. You know I haven't. I would've told you if I had. Why? Has someone seen her?'

There's a pause. It's so frustrating that I can't see what's going on.

'I don't think this is a conversation I want to have while standing in the corridor.'

I hear the front door open wider and step back, hand against the wall, leaning into it. I know he doesn't know I'm here. I don't think he does anyway. But every cell in my body is just screaming at me to leave.

Not that I can do that. I have to stay. I have to get the answers I need.

I hear Josh's voice again. 'So, what's happened?'

'Carly saw her at the library. She gave her my card. Rhiannon rang us but wouldn't come in.'

'Why wouldn't she come in?'

I lean closer again, wondering what he's going to say, and I see a body walk past the door before I jerk back. The quick glance I had was of grey – grey hair, grey suit, grey shoes. Charles. My father.

'We believe she may have suffered a form of amnesia.'

'She's lost her memory?' I can hear the fake confusion in Josh's voice. He's a good actor. I wonder what he's lied to *me* about. 'Why would you think that?'

'It doesn't matter why I think it. Have you seen her?' He sounds angry. Or maybe frustrated is better.

A flicker of satisfaction shoots through me. Yep, definitely a bitch. And I'm okay with that.

'I told you, no. If I'd seen her, I would've brought her in.'

There's another pause. This one goes on so long it makes me want to scream. Which sort of defeats the whole reason for hiding.

Charles is the first to speak. His voice is so low and quiet I have to strain to hear it.

'I would hope so. I would hope that you wouldn't let this so-called engagement with my daughter ruin the agreement we have.'

I take a step back. So-called! What the hell does that mean? And what agreement? I feel sick – my stomach rolling, twisting. Would the me before all this know what that meant? Or would she have been feeling just as confused? Can I trust Josh? We were engaged. Or maybe not. Maybe that was a lie too, like Charles said. I close my eyes and lean my forehead on the wall. God! Just as I think I'm getting a handle on everything, it twists and changes, like the earth is buckling under me.

Josh's voice is just as terse as Charles's.

'I said I'd bring her in if I saw her. You have no reason not to trust me.'

'No. I don't suppose I have. At the moment. See that it stays that way.'

I hear footsteps moving towards the door – Charles I'm guessing, but I stay where I am anyway, just in case. It's not until I hear the clicking of the lock that I move towards the bedroom door. I open it just as Josh gets there. We're close – close enough that I could lean forward and kiss him. But I don't. I just look at him. He looks back. There's no smile, no teasing.

'Are you going to take me in now?'

The grimace on his face gets deeper.

'No, I'm not going to take you in. Christ, Rhi. What a question! If I was going to do that, I would have done it as soon as I saw you on the street.'

I nod. He has a point. I want to ask him about the agreement, about the so-called engagement but I just can't. How stupid is it that I don't really want to know? I want him. I want him to want me. For a little while there, it was nice to feel like I belonged somewhere. That I had someone who cared about me and what happened to me.

'Come on. We have to get out of here. You can bet Charles will be back.'

'Where are we going?'

He rolls his eyes at the tone of my voice.

'Not back to RACE. I'm going to take you to your place.'

'My place?'

'Yeah. It's about ten blocks from here. I'm guessing you haven't been back there yet?'

I shake my head, blinking away what feels suspiciously like tears. How much easier would this have been if I'd been able to zap there? Stupid brain or whatever it is that's been streaming me everywhere.

He takes my hand and I let it happen. The desire to see my home overrides my concerns about him. For the moment.

'Do you trust me with this? Trust me to take you there?' he says.

I want to say yes. But I can't. So I don't say anything.

He sighs. 'Guess I'll have to prove it to you then.'

And we are gone.

CHAPTER 15

I know this place as soon as we get there. The connection is so strong – so comforting – that a sob breaks away from me before I can stop it. I put my hand over my mouth, holding back any more. I let go of Josh's hand and look around me. It's not a large room but I love it.

Three huge windows in the main living area, framed in light timber, look out over a park. It is light and airy, even in the fading afternoon light. I run my hand over the back of the lime green sofa – the only splash of colour in a white room.

'You searched for months before you found that sofa.'

My eyes flick to Josh and I nod but I can't talk. If I do, all the emotion that's sitting inside me will come rushing out, overwhelming me. It's all I can do to keep it under control now.

I can see the bedroom through a partially opened door and go over to it, pushing it with my fingertips. I stand at the threshold, taking it all in. There's a white timber bed pushed up against the far wall, piled high with cushions in various shades of blues and greens. A white egg chair sits against the window, open to the view, perfect for reading. And on the adjacent wall is a chest of draws, the top littered with photos. Photos of my life. I walk over but it feels like I'm part of a dream. Any moment now, I'm going to wake up and this will all be gone.

I rest my hand on the edge of the dresser, almost afraid to touch the frames. It's like I don't know where to start. It's only when he places a hand gently on my shoulder that I realise Josh is behind me. I startle and he rubs my skin. It feels awesome and annoying, all at the same time. I want him here but I want to do this by myself as well. Or maybe I don't really know what I want. So I let him leave it there.

Josh reaches out and takes a frame from the side. It is one of him and me, smiling, looking happy. Like we're in love. I could believe these two people were engaged. Truly. Not a 'so-called' engagement, whatever that means.

'This was taken at the beginning of the year,' he says. 'You were trying to teach me to fish but I was terrible at it. You shouted me fish and chips on the way home instead. It was a good day.'

I shut my eyes, trying to focus on the myriad of

pictures that are suddenly flicking through my head, like a photo album on speed.

'At the jetty.'

He squeezes my shoulder. 'That's right.'

I squeeze my lips shut, tight, and move away so that his hand falls.

'What's wrong?'

I shake my head, not looking at him. He wraps me in an embrace.

'Rhi, what is it? You remembered something. That's good. Right?'

I nod and then shake my head.

'What?'

'What if I can't remember anything else? What if that's it? What if whatever's happened to me can't be fixed?'

He hugs me tighter.

'Hey, it's a start. Don't worry, I'll help you.'

I want to trust him. Really, truly, honest-to-God want to believe him. Even though what Charles said to him keeps running around in my brain, planting seeds everywhere. So I don't ask the question that needs to be asked. I just enjoy the feelings of his arms around me. For the moment, that's what I need.

I'm not sure how long we stand like that before he pulls away.

'Listen, why don't you go and have a shower and change your clothes. It'll make you feel better. Then I can tell you the rest of what I know.'

I raise my eyebrows. 'What? Are you trying to tell me I stink?'

He grins at me. 'I'm a gentleman. I'd never tell you that. It was you who said it.'

I whack him with my hand and he does a half-assed effort at defending himself before grabbing my wrist, twirling me around, and tapping my butt, sending me towards a door in the opposite wall.

'Go on.'

I step away and laugh. The thought of a shower does sound like bliss. I open the door – the ensuite, as I suspected – and turn back to him.

'Will Charles come looking for me here? I mean, he came to your place. Won't this be the next logical place he'll look?'

Josh shakes his head.

'This place isn't registered in your name. Your Grandma – your mum's mum – owned it. She gave you this place when she moved into the nursing home, just before she died. You used to spend a lot of time here when you were a kid. I doubt you ever told your Dad though. You weren't what you'd call close, even though you worked for him. I'm pretty sure he still thinks you live with your mum.'

I frown. 'My own father doesn't know where I live?'

Josh raises his eyebrows. 'Why? Are you thinking about telling him?'

I actually shudder at that thought. 'God no!'

'See, your gut still knows the right thing to do.'

'He's a piece of work, huh?'

Josh does a lopsided smile – only one half of his lips quirking up. It makes me want to kiss him. I hold tighter onto the door frame.

'You could say that.'

'So why do you still work for him?'

'The same reason you did. The chance to do good. And the money's not bad. But no more questions. Go and have a shower and then I'll tell you everything.'

I stick my tongue out at him and start to go before turning around again.

'What will I do if I stream out while I'm in here? How will I get back to you?'

'You can always come back here now you know it. I'll find you here.'

'But what if I can't do it. Pick where I want to go, I mean.'

My short dip in the fountain isn't enough to fill me with confidence that I can do it again. And the thought of going back to streaming with no control is enough to make me nauseous.

He frowns. 'Okay, well let's do a test. The green couch – I want you to take yourself out there.'

'How do I do that?'

He looks perplexed for a moment. 'Umm, well, why don't you close your eyes to start? That'll probably make it easier.' I shut my eyes, like a good little girl. 'Then focus on the couch – like you're already out there. Picture yourself standing there. Got it?'

I nod. I can feel the energy moving around in me already, like I've woken a sleeping beast.

'Okay then bring the energy towards you like you're holding it in a ball in the centre of your chest and push it out, quick, like it's bursting out of your skin.'

He sounds more confident with the last part, like he knows what he's doing. Still, it's scary. What if it doesn't work? I take a deep breath, collecting all the power in me and moving it until it's a ball of electricity sitting in the middle of my chest. I focus on the couch – where it is in the room, how the fabric felt under my skin – picture myself standing there. I push the energy out, flinging it away from me.

I wobble slightly, off-balance, and use the arm of the couch to stabilise me. I am here. I did it!

Josh is standing at the door, a big grin splitting his gorgeous face. I can't help but smile back.

'I did it!'

'You sure did.'

I nod, just once, short and sharp.

'And now I can take that shower.'

He stops me as I walk past and brushes his lips over mine. A tease. I want more instantly. More of him. But I don't know that I'm ready for that. Not yet. I push against him.

'A shower and then we talk.'

He runs his hand down my arm. 'Your wish is my command.'

'Stop doing that.'

'What?'

'Trying to distract me.'

He laughs and raises one eyebrow. 'Is it working?'

If I was being truthful I'd tell him yes. 'You wish.'

And I force myself to move away from his touch. I close the bathroom door with a little more force than I need and lean against it for a moment, taking a deep breath. Trying to slow my heart down. I wonder if it's always been like this between us. If it was, I'm not sure how we ever got anything done.

Now that I finally have the opportunity, I can't wait to get out of these clothes. Four days of dirt and sweat and death feel like they've soaked into the material and I want to get them away from my body. I don't think I'll even worry about washing them, just throw them away. I take the money, Charles's card and the photo from my pocket and put them on the bench before shedding my clothes as quickly as I can.

The water is hot and I let it run over me, soaking me, washing away the effects of all the experiences I remember as well as the ones that happened before I lost my memory. I want to feel fresh and clean and… free. It sounds stupid but it's what I need.

I shampoo my hair, letting the suds run down my skin, and then shampoo it again. Maybe I could just stay in here, under the water, rather than facing all the unknowns that are waiting for me. How nice would that be? Actually, no it would be better if I didn't have any of these question marks over my life to start with – if I hadn't lost my memory and everything was normal. Except then, obviously, I wouldn't be spending this time with Josh. And that thought makes my stomach curl up in knots. Which doesn't make sense. If I broke up with him, then something was wrong between us. Something more than me not wanting to commit – surely I can't be that shallow.

I turn off the water and rub myself with the towel until my skin is red before lathering my body in the cream on the bench – lemon myrtle. I love the smell, even if I didn't remember that I did love it until this moment. I run my fingers through my hair, shaping it into place, and brush my teeth. It's only when I do that that I realise how bad my breath must have smelled. And yet, Josh has been willing to kiss me.

I hold my gaze in the mirror for a moment, trying to think about what I need to do. Trying to decide if I can trust him. Because I still can't get Charles's words out of my head. God, how can he be my father? He seems like such a horrible person. My instincts tell me that he is horrible, even if I can't remember what he's done.

I lean forward and put my forehead against the cold glass of the mirror, closing my eyes. It's time for answers. Time to get this sorted in my head, even if it doesn't make me remember everything about my life, I need to at least know what I'm facing.

I wrap the towel around me and crack open the door. Josh is there, on my bed, spread out like it's his second home. Maybe it is. Or was. I step out, holding the towel tight, feeling like an idiot. But even if he's seen me naked before I can't remember it. And this is my room.

He opens his eyes as I walk out.

'Feel better?'

I nod but he doesn't get up.

'Can you get out?'

He smiles. 'I could.'

He puts his hands behind his head, looking at me. But that's the only movement he makes.

'Josh, come on. I need to get dressed.'

He grins. 'You've got dressed in front of me plenty of times before.'

'Yeah, well that was before. Get the hell out.'

'What if I promise to close my eyes?'

'I can't believe we're having this conversation. Get out.'

He sighs but swings his legs over the side of the bed.

'God, I can't wait til you get your memory back.'

'Yeah well, you and me both. Get out.'

I step back as he goes past and he grins again but keeps on going, closing the door with exaggerated care behind him. I don't waste any time finding clothes. It's not like I have a huge choice anyway. Obviously, clothes aren't an obsession for me. Which is great because it means it's easy to make a quick decision. Underwear – both black, black shorts, blue top. I don't even bother to look in the mirror. It's time to talk.

CHAPTER 16

Josh has turned the lights on and is standing in the kitchen, stirring something in mugs. He pushes one towards me.

'Tea, black, one sugar.'

'Is that how I like it?'

'Yep.'

Another thing to add to the growing list of facts about myself. I take a sip – it's hot but good. I put it down, turning the handle so it's parallel with the bench. Wasting time, even though I don't know if I have that luxury.

'Time for answers, huh?' Josh is looking at me with a softness in his eyes. Like he can see right through me. Like he knows about the rolling in my stomach, how tight my chest is.

I want answers and yet, I don't know that I really

do want them. How can it be possible to want something so badly but want to run away from it at the same time? My father obviously isn't a particularly nice guy. My brother – well, God knows – all I've got is this huge wave of anxiety that washes over me every time I think about him. And even this gorgeous man in front of me – the one that makes me forget about finding out about myself and think more about what sex would be like with him – even he has question marks. Jesus. I rub my eyes.

'Yep, answers. That's what I need.'

'Okay. Ask your questions then.'

I don't know where to start. My brain is so empty the amount of information I need to fill it up is overwhelming. I don't know if it's the fact that I don't answer him or if it's the expression on my face but Josh pushes my chin up with his fingers so that I'm looking at him.

'Hey. Don't stress. There's time.'

I nod but I still can't think of which question to ask first. He sits on the stool next to me.

'Let's see. Your birthday is the fourth of August. You're twenty – so all good, haven't missed your twenty-first. You hate strawberries but love brussel sprouts – weirdest thing ever. You had a dog named Jack that died last year. He still lived with your mum. Favourite colour is green. You love to read. If you exercise, you prefer to swim. You prefer tea over coffee. You sleep on the left side of the bed and don't really like spooning. You eat your cereal with no milk. And you think I'm pretty awesome.'

He grins at me but I can't grin back. All I can focus on is the fact that he knows so much about me. Little things. Things that means he cares. About me…Or that he's a really good stalker. I think I prefer the first explanation. His grin fades as I just stare at him.

'What?'

I shake my head. 'I can't believe you remember all that.'

'Of course I do. I love you. Even though we aren't together anymore.' He plays with his cup and then looks up at me. 'I know that probably sounds weird. But I still do. I just wanted you to know. I think I have from the first moment I saw you, when I came to work at RACE.'

I don't know what to say to this declaration. I want to reach out, touch his hand, kiss him, but the unknown is stopping me. The past me – well, she must have had a good reason to end it. Except it sort of feels like I love him too…still.

I ignore the urge and ask the only safe question I can.

'When was that?'

'Eighteen months ago. You'd been there about three months before I started. You told me you didn't want to be – not at first. I think you were pretty pissed at your dad and resisted going to work there, even though he was begging you. It was Adam that convinced you in the end.'

Adam. The name hangs in the air, enveloping me, tugging at my soul in a way that makes my heart hurt. I want to ask more questions but it still feels too big, like I'm poking at a wound, despite what Josh said before. Not yet. I'm being a coward.

'And why did he want me to join so badly?'

'Streamers are hard to come by. And you and Adam both got it from him. He's a streamer too.'

'My mum isn't?'

'No.' He pauses like he's trying to work out what to say next. It has my antennae on high alert. 'She….didn't like streaming. And she didn't want your dad anywhere near you. At least that's what you told me. She was pretty angry when he left.'

'When was that?' It's weird that he knows more about my childhood than me.

'I think when you were about three.'

Three. I wonder what happened to them to make them split up.

'What's she like? My mum?'

His mouth thins into a grimace.

'I haven't actually met her.'

'But?'

'Well, she's an alcoholic.' He frowns. 'Shit. Sorry. That sounds bad.'

'No. It's okay. I need to know.' Even though I

don't really want to. I want to put my hands over my ears and go 'la la la'.

He plays with the coffee mug again. I want to move it away from him, tell him to focus, but maybe it's me that needs to do that.

'You haven't seen her since you started working for Charles. You told me that she said if you go to him, you wouldn't be welcome back home.'

Well, that explains the reaction I got from her. And how gaunt she looked.

'So she just cut me out of her life?'

He nods. 'I don't think it was a really good life though. You said she used to be passed out most of the time. Not abusive necessarily…just neglectful. Adam used to do a lot of things for you.'

Adam. We're back to my brother. My protector. Was Mum one of the things he was protecting me from? It feels right. But maybe that's because Josh is saying it – maybe it's just easier to believe him than try to find my own memories. I don't know. I rub my face. I don't want to talk about my mum anymore. Or Adam.

'What else? How did Charles find you? How did you know he was looking for streamers?'

'I didn't know. But he recognised the power in me when I streamed into the restaurant he was in one day. We can feel the power in each other. Did you feel it in me? And in Carly, at the library?'

I nod. There was something about both of them

– something that drew me too them, even if I didn't know what it was.

'What do we do at RACE?'

'We're…problem solvers. At least that's what Charles calls us anyway.'

'What the hell does that mean?'

'It means people come to us with certain things they want done. An item retrieved, information gathered, someone delayed maybe…things like that.'

I can feel the frown settle on my forehead.

'What do you mean? Did we steal things? Are we thieves or something?'

I need him to say no. I can't have been that person – not willingly! I let out the breath that I didn't realise I was holding when he shakes his head.

'Shit no! People needed to provide proof that they owned something or that there's a moral reason for wanting the information. It has to be above board. As much as we can make it anyway. One of your first jobs was to bring back a kid who'd been taken overseas by his dad. His mum was never going to see him again, even though she had custody. You were pretty stoked about that. We did good things.'

'Did?'

He shrugs and suddenly looks uncomfortable, like the seat's grown spikes that are sticking into him.

'Like I said, Charles has been wired lately. Manic. Saying that we have to be ready to meet the market on a wider scope, that we need to commit to use the resources we have…blah, blah, blah. If I didn't know better, I'd say he's become the evil overlord type.'

He laughs but it doesn't sound like he finds it funny. God.

'That's one of the reasons I didn't tell him when I found you. It's also why I was looking for you so hard. I just don't trust him anymore. Not like I used to anyway.'

'How long?'

'How long what?'

'How long has he been like this?'

'Really like this? Probably the last six months.'

I take a deep breath and put one hand on the bench, gripping it, feeling the cool of the granite under my fingertips – cold in comparison to the heat that's taking over my body.

'And how have I reacted to that.' It seems like a weird thing to ask.

He frowns. 'I don't know. You haven't really said anything. It's weird actually. It's like you haven't even noticed.'

'How is that possible?'

'I don't know. I haven't thought about it until now. But it's something you'd usually comment on.'

It feels like there's so much about the last few months that's a mystery. Frustratingly buried. God, I want to curl into a ball on my bed and sleep until everything comes back!

But that's not an option. I need to know. I want to fill in the blank spaces.

I stand, moving to between his legs, smoothing away the frown lines on his forehead. His hands come around my backside, pulling me in. It feels nice. Safe. Safe enough that I can be brave and ask the next question.

'What happened to me? How did I lose my memory?'

His hand comes up to cup my cheek and he looks sad.

'I don't know.'

CHAPTER 17

I'm lying in the dim light given off by the bedside lamp, staring at the ceiling. The photos from the top of my chest of drawers are spread out on the covers around me. I've been looking at them, willing them to tease my memories back to life but there's been nothing. No flickering of times in the past, no glimpses of my life. Nothing.

Josh is lying next to me – I can hear his steady breath, which is really bugging me. How can he have the luxury of being asleep – of being able to not think about things for a moment – while I lie here with my thoughts in a whirl?

I'm not tired – far from it. The only reason I'm in bed rather than doing someone proactive is because Josh was starting to wilt. And now I can't stop thinking about that. How is it that he's a streamer too and yet can't do the same draining energy thing? And if it wasn't something I did before, what's happened to me? Obviously that and the memory loss are connected. They must be. I wish I could remember! Sort of ironic really...

I turn my head to look at Josh. His skin looks almost golden in the soft light. Like honey. Good enough to lick. His arm is above his head and he looks peaceful. Arsehole!

I want to trust him. More than anything, I want to be able to know that there's someone whose motives I don't have to think about on top of everything else. But doubt is still ricocheting around in my head, dinting everything that he says to me – making me question it, poke at it. I huff out a lung full of air and look back up at the ceiling.

There's a shift in the bed next to me. An alertness. He's awake.

'Are you okay?'

'Oh, sure, yeah. Can't remember my life, have a psycho father, an alcoholic mother, a brother who I'm pretty sure something's happened to and yet, no one knows where he is, and I can drain the energy out of people until they're dead. So essentially, I'm a killer. Everything is just peachy keen.'

There's silence for a second and then he rolls over, pushing the frames out of the way until he's hugging into me, pulling me closer.

'We'll work it out.'

I'm silent while he holds me. The feel of his fingers on my waist, the smell of his skin – I want to think this is real…

I don't know if it's my silence or the fact that I'm not holding him back that clues him in but he sighs and sits up, looking down at me.

His hair is disheveled and he roughs it up even more as he runs his fingers through it. I wonder if he knows how sexy that makes him look. He's in a pair of boxers that he pulled out of one of the draws in my apartment, which must tell me something. Mustn't it? The fact that his stuff is still here even though we'd broken up. Maybe it just tells me I was a sucker before all of this…

I want to run my fingers down his bare chest – feel my nails gently trace his skin – leave my mark, even if it's only a temporary thing. I grip the sheets with my fingers instead.

'Okay,' he says. 'What's bugging you? There's something more than just …well, than just this memory thing, isn't there?'

I stay silent, even though I want to get it out into the open; clear things up. Because I'm torn between that and just wanting to curl into a ball and pretend I'm asleep. My heart is thumping as I look at him and I'm trying to work out why it's so important that he says the right things – makes me believe in him.

'Come on Rhi. What is it?'

'Nothing.'

'Bullshit. I know you. What's wrong?'

How can he know me when I don't even know myself? It's so unfair. Irrational sure, but still damn unfair! I sit up too but I'm still shorter than him so I get up onto my knees so we're even in height.

'All right then. What did Charles mean when he came to your apartment?'

He frowns. 'What did Charles mean with what?'

But he's not looking at me. His eyes keep flicking away and then back.

'Don't act stupid. It doesn't suit you.'

He sighs again and sags down a little.

'The comment about the so-called engagement and the agreement?'

I smirk, even though inside, it feels like I'm being carved up, slowly and meticulously, with a scalpel. 'That's it.'

'I was wondering if you heard that.'

It feels like he's stalling for time. The carving is getting worse. I don't answer him.

'Shit, Rhi. It's nothing. Just your dad being a dickhead.'

I'm silent still. He rubs his hair again and then lets his hands fall to the mattress.

'When I first starting working at RACE, your dad asked me to keep an eye on you.'

'Why?'

'Because he was worried you might do something

stupid as a sort of revenge thing on him not being around when you were a kid. Something stupid that'd hurt the business.'

So worried about the business then – not me. My father just keeps getting better and better.

'And did I?'

He shakes his head.

'Your brother tried to tell your dad you'd be fine but he didn't believe him.'

Adam. My heart rate increases again and I put my hand against my chest, as if that will make it slow down.

'What did keeping an eye on me mean?'

He looks away, down at the sheet, and plucks at it with his fingers.

'Don't, Rhi. Just leave it. Please.' His voice is husky, pleading.

'Tell me.'

He looks up at the ceiling, like it has the answer written there. It doesn't – I've already looked.

'He wanted me to make you like me.'

My mouth is suddenly dry – arid-desert-after-no-rain-for-ten-years dry.

'As in, 'like you' like you?'

He looks at me then. I can see the pleading in his eyes…begging me not to ask any more questions. Fat chance of that.

'So it's all fake then. You only like me because

Charles told you too. Actually, you may not even like me! Maybe it's all just an act!'

He grabs my hand. I try to pull away but he holds on, his fingers pressing into my skin. I stop pulling and let my hand go limp.

'I love you. You know that.'

'No actually, I don't! I'm only going on what you've told me.'

'You're saying you don't feel anything for me then?'

I am so not answering that question. I narrow my eyes at him instead.

'Did I know about your deal with him before I lost my memory?'

His silence is all the answer I need.

'God! What did he promise you? What was he going to give you for making me fucking fall in love with you?'

He shakes his head.

'What did he promise you, Josh?'

He sighs. 'Adam was thinking about leaving. Charles said he'd make me second in charge – make me a partner. Which meant more money.'

'Jesus, how clichéd can you get? You sold me out for money and power. Fuck! Calling my father a piece of work…you're just as bad! I can't believe I fell for it.'

'I agreed before I even knew you. But it doesn't

mean anything. I couldn't care less about any of it. I love you.'

'Sure! And how am I supposed to trust in that?'

'I didn't tell Charles you were in the unit. I kept you safe.'

I can't argue with that. I feel like I should, just to prove a point, but I'm not actually sure I want the point proven. Am I so needy that I'm willing to still be with him even though he's played me? Or to believe that he hasn't played me at all…that he really loves me?

Because if I'm being honest, I still want him – want to be with him, want him to love me, want to be in his arms. And I think I'm still in love with him, despite the fact that I dumped him. I'm a wussy girl. A bitch, sure, but a wussy female to go with it.

'Please,' he says, leaning forward, touching my knee. It sends a jolt through me, like a charge that makes each cell revel at his touch. Traitors. 'You have to believe me. How I feel about you has got nothing to do with Charles. It might have in the first place but it didn't stay that way, not once I got to know you.'

He stares at me, not breathing, waiting for my answer. I don't know what to tell him. I ask a question instead.

'Why did we really break up?'

He shakes his head. 'I told you. I don't know. You

just came over and you were all hyped up – you didn't want to sit down or kiss me – you just paced around the unit. I tried to hug you and you almost jumped out of your skin. And you said you didn't want to do this anymore. You said you were too young to commit and that you just wanted to have some fun.'

I frown. 'Was that usual behaviour for me?'

'No! I didn't know what was going on. I was totally shocked. And panicked. I couldn't work out what had happened. But when I tried to talk to you about it, you said there was nothing to talk about and that it was the end of it. And then you left.'

He blinks, like he's trying to hold back tears. 'Please, Rhi, I'm telling you the truth. I didn't do anything. I love you.'

I nod. It's a distracted one. I'm trying to fit this information into place but the connecting parts – the information that would make it make sense – the important stuff…it's all still missing.

He touches me again.

'Do you think we can start again?'

Yes. That's what I want to say. But I don't know. Not for sure. How can I trust that he's telling me the truth?

'I don't know.'

He lets out a shaky breath and bitch that I am, I sort of like that it means that much to him. Maybe he really does love me.

'Okay. At least that's not a no.'

I'm saved from having to say anything else by the ringing of the phone. It's Josh's, flashing on the bedside table. He looks at it and then back at me.

'Answer it.'

He grabs it and his face is grim.

'It's your father.'

He puts the phone on speaker – to try and prove he's got nothing to hide, I guess – and I make sure I'm quiet.

'Hello.'

'Joshua. I need you in here straight away.'

'It's the middle of the night!'

'I don't care. I tell you to come, you come.'

'I'm on holidays, remember? What's so important that someone else can't do it?'

There is a pause so long I wonder if Charles has actually just got the shits and hung up. Finally, his voice echoes over the line.

'It's about Adam.'

And then he hangs up.

Adam. Adam. Adam…his name ricochets in my head and I lean back on the headboard, looking at Josh. He still has the phone in his hand and he's flipping it round and round, staring into space.

'Tell me.'

He shakes his head. 'I don't really know anything else.'

'Josh.'

'Truly, I told you all of what I know before. No

one's seen him in a while but apparently he's been staying at the office and Charles hasn't been worried so neither has anyone else.'

I wait for the rest. He tries to last me out but I'm more determined than him – maybe I have more at stake. Or maybe I'm just stubborn.

'Christ, Rhi, the only other part is a rumour. I don't know if it's true or not.'

'What's the rumour?'

'You're not going to let this go, are you?'

'I can't.'

He shuts his eyes like I'm causing him pain and then sighs.

'Okay, the rumour is that he did a job and that something happened to him either there or coming back – something in the stream. They're saying he's sick. Really sick. And that Charles is trying to make him better. But I didn't want to tell you that because I didn't think it was true.'

Adam. Sick? God!

'Well, apparently something's up for Charles to want you to come in.'

I get up and start to pace, needing to do something apart from sitting on the bed. This is it – this is why I've been feeling bad. I must have known something about this, even though I can't remember what it is now. Jesus, why can't I just remember?

The chest of drawers still has some photos on it and I look through them, tipping them over in my haste before opening the drawers and rummaging through them.

'What are you doing?'

I don't bother turning back to face Josh.

'A photo of Adam. I must have one. A recent one.'

He comes over and puts his hand on my arm.

'There's a photo album in the lounge room.'

I follow him out and he goes to the low, white cabinet that the TV sits on and pulls a photo album out of one of the drawers. I sit on the couch and put it on my lap, running my hands over the front cover for a moment before opening it, flicking through the pages quickly, like I need to get it over and done with.

It's full of photos of my life – family, places I've been, friends, Josh. It's almost too much and I shut my eyes for a moment, letting the tightness of my chest ease slightly. Enough that I feel like I can breathe again. Then I start back at the beginning. On the second page, there's a photo of me – I look about seventeen or so – and of a man. He looks enough like the other boy in the photo I took from Mum's to know it's Adam. He's still not smiling. Serious, loving, protective. My big brother.

I run my finger over his face. Memories hit me in a burst of colour and sound. I can hear his voice, remember the way his mouth quirks up at the side when he actually does smile. I remember him being there for me when the two parents I had turned out to be pretty shit at it. And I can remember him hugging me when Dad came back into our life. He was a lot more forgiving than I was. But he'd known Dad for longer before he left. Maybe that made a difference.

Josh breaks into my memories. His voice is soft, like he doesn't want to. 'I have to go. Charles will be expecting me.'

I nod. 'I'm coming with you.'

'Rhi, that's not a good idea. I don't know what happened to you but if it's got anything to do with Charles, then it's stupid for you to come. God, whatever happened was enough to make you lose your memory and send you off in some random streaming nightmare with no idea what you were doing. What if Charles sees you? Shit! Let's work out what happened first, okay?'

I put the photo album down on the lounge beside me. Part of me is amazed that he's still trying to talk me out of things – maybe he doesn't know me as well as he says he does. Or maybe he's an optimist.

'I don't care. This is about Adam. I'm coming.'

He grips my hand and looks hard at me.

'I'm directing us then. We can't just appear in the middle of the office. Let me lead.'

'Okay, whatever. As long as we're there.'

He looks at me for a moment like he doesn't believe me and I raise my eyebrows. Finally, he sighs.

'And then, when we're in there, you need to do what I tell you.'

I laugh. 'Don't get too hopeful.'

He rolls his eyes.

'You ready?'

I nod and he nods back. Then we're gone.

CHAPTER 18

We're in a bathroom. The women's bathroom I'm guessing from the lack of urinals lining the wall. I turn to Josh, leaning close so that he can hear me without my voice carrying.

'This is where you thought to bring us?'

He shrugs.

'You're the only female streamer working here at the moment. And I thought we'd be pretty safe at this time of night.'

I nod, trying to ignore the shivers that are travelling down my spine at his breath on my neck. Not the time or place.

'Let's go.'

He holds me back.

'Let me go and see what's going on first. I'll come back and get you when I know it's safe.'

I'm shaking my head before he finishes talking.

'Please, Rhi. Five minutes, that's all I'm asking.'

He looks so worried I don't have the heart to tell him to get stuffed.

'Fine. Five minutes and then I'm out of here whether you're back or not.'

He grimaces but nods anyway. And look at me, compromising. Another thing I've found out about myself. He lets go of my hand and opens the door slightly, looking out, before turning back.

'Five minutes,' I say and he nods.

I go into one of the cubicles, just in case he's wrong and someone does come in, and watch the seconds tick away on my watch, each one an eternity. My muscles feel like they're stretched as tight as the skin of a blown-up balloon. I wait for the door to open….waiting for Josh to come back and tell me it's okay.

I can hardly believe it when the hand ticks past five minutes and there's no sign of him. It didn't even really cross my mind that he wouldn't be here. Helping me. How stupid is it that I'm relying on him? I shake my head – I don't need him. What am I thinking? Sure, it'd probably be easier given there's lots I can't remember but I can do this on my own.

I open the door of the cubicle, just a fraction – no point in being stupid. The bathroom is still empty. My shoes make a light tapping sound on the tiles and I walk on my toes to minimise it. I stop at the door and take a deep breath, trying to slow my heart, calming the energy that's pulsing through my body, still trying to pull me away. But it can't anymore – I know how to control it.

There's no one in the hallway when I open the door. It goes in either direction in a curve and the doors I can see are all shut. I have no clue which way I should take. Left then, for no other reason than that sounds good.

I listen at the doors as I pass but there's no sound from behind any of them. I keep waiting for someone to come out and see me though. Even the fact that it's the middle of the night and there's a good chance that there's hardly anyone here doesn't stop my brain imagining discovery, infecting my body with its stress.

I can see a kitchen at the end of the hallway but, before that, the last door on the right is open. And I can hear voices coming from it. I stand flat to the wall just beside the door frame and listen.

Josh's voice. And Charles's. And another person. He sounds familiar, even if I can't picture him. Adam, maybe? And yet, that doesn't feel right. Someone else then. Someone I know through RACE. I'm so tempted to put my head around and look into the room that I'm actually starting to turn before I stop myself. Stupid.

I listen instead. Even if Josh tells me everything later, I'd rather hear it myself. Now. Patience doesn't feel like it's one of my strong points. And if I listen, I won't get Josh's sanitised version.

'I'm not doing it!' Josh sounds angry. No, more than that. Really pissed.

'You'll do what I tell you.'

'Bullshit! You're my boss, not a frigging God. Get over yourself.'

The other man is talking now. 'I think we need to calm down. This can't be the only option, Charles.'

'You've seen him, Richard. You've seen what he's like. If we leave him like that, there's no telling what he'll do.'

I grit my teeth, wanting to scream. Are they talking about Adam? They must be. But what the hell does that mean?

'And whose fault is it that he's like that?' Josh doesn't sound like he's calmed down at all. 'What have you done to him? Jesus, you're his fucking father and you've left him like that!'

'I haven't done anything that he didn't agree to. Nothing that he didn't want to try himself. I'm not looking for your judgment, just your loyalty.'

'You're asking me for more than that. Fuck! Did you try this shit on Rhi too? Is that why she left? Why we can't find her?'

There's anger in Charles's voice when he answers. Enough that it makes me draw back slightly, further along the wall. 'What has happened to Rhiannon has nothing to do with you.'

'Are you fucking kidding me? We were engaged! I was going to marry her!'

'Yes, well, those plans changed, didn't they? She told me she'd broken it off with you.'

I don't know if that comment makes me angry or scared. Probably a bit of both. Because why would I tell my father about my personal life when I haven't even told him where I live? Especially when it only happened the day before I disappeared. It doesn't make sense.

'Listen, I think we need to focus on Adam. There has to be another way. You can't ask Josh to terminate him. Jesus, we help people, we don't kill them!' It's the other man – Richard.

'Always soft.' Charles's voice is filled with contempt. 'How do you expect us to grow this business, make it the premium fixing agency of the world, the place that everyone – governments, private businesses, people with money and power – will come to, to have their issues sorted if you won't make the difficult decisions, Richard?'

'Why don't you do it then?' Josh's voice is louder, like he's moved closer to the door. 'You kill him.'

'I can't do that. We're blood. The power he can exert over me doubles, triples, because of that blood connection.'

Josh snorts. 'Well, that's fucking convenient!'

The room is silent and I can barely stop myself from looking inside to see what's going on. But I can't believe what I'm hearing. He wants to kill Adam! His own son! The evilness of it is too big to get my head around. All I know for sure is that I can't let him do it. I need to find Adam and take him away and make him safe! And I need to make sure that whatever Charles has done to Adam doesn't happen to me. Because maybe Josh is right – maybe Charles is the reason I've lost my memory. Maybe Charles is the reason I can kill someone by taking their energy.

I double back down the hall, past the bathrooms and turn the corner. The rest of the offices are in the dark and I stop for a moment to let my eyes adjust.

When a hand clasps over my mouth, I react without even thinking. Their energy begins to flow into me before I even begin to struggle.

'Rhi, it's me! Stop!'

Josh!

I draw back from the power, snapping it off like breaking a stick in half. God! How has this become my 'go to' move to protect myself? What's happened to my brain that this is what I resort to?

I turn out of his hands, glaring at him. Not that I'm angry really – scared, anxious, frustrated – take your pick. But anger is easier.

'What the hell are you doing? Jesus!' It's hard to show how angry you are when you're whispering.

'I came to find you. You're lucky it's me that saw you and not Charles.'

I look up at him but his face is highlighted from the back, making it hard to read his expression.

'Did he really ask you to kill Adam?'

He pushes me back, further in the shadows, using the wall to protect us from view.

'You heard that then?'

I raise my eyebrows, even though he probably can't see them.

'Five minutes, Josh. Did you really think I'd wait when you didn't come back?'

He chuckles and touches my cheek with the back of his hand.

'God, I love you.'

I want to say it back – the words feel like they're sitting in my mouth, waiting to come out, but I swallow them back down. Not when we still haven't worked out what happened between us. Later… maybe…when we've had a chance to talk more.

'Are you going to do it?'

'Jesus, Rhi, how can you even ask that? Of course I'm not going to kill him!'

I reach out to touch his hand.

'Are you okay? Did I drain too much energy?'

'No, I'm okay.'

'We need to find Adam.'

'I know where he is.'

'Great. Let's go.'

I start down the hallway, even though I've got no idea where I'm going. But I need to get moving. I need to get there before Charles does. Or before Charles convinces someone else to kill my brother.

'Rhi, wait.'

'No. No more waiting. I've waited long enough.'

'He's not the Adam you remember.'

I laugh, even though it's not really funny.

'Don't worry, I don't really remember much anyway.'

'Christ, I'm sorry. That's not what I meant.'

I shake my head. 'It doesn't matter.'

'Yes, it does. He's not the same. He's not the Adam I know. He's dangerous.'

'What does that mean?'

'Look, don't take this the wrong way, but he's like you, on steroids.'

'What?' I want him to stop talking in riddles – I'm sick of mysteries.

'Charles said he can drain energy, just like you, I guess. But he doesn't have, I don't know, a control switch. A way to stop it like you just did with me. Charles said it happens whether he wants it to or not.'

'He's my brother. He's not going to hurt me.' I can hear the stubbornness in my voice.

'It's not like that.'

'Just show me where he is or I'll find him myself.'

He shakes his head, face raised to the ceiling likes he's struggling with this decision.

I touch his arm. 'Please. I need to see him.'

He sighs and rolls his eyes. 'Always so frigging stubborn. Fine. This way.'

He takes my arm and leads me further down the hall. When he stops and turns to me, taking my hands in his, I'm pretty sure he's going to try and talk me out of going again. I go to open my mouth but he puts his fingers to my lips before can I say anything.

'We have to stream there. Trust me?'

That's such a complicated question, full of the past and the unknown and the forgotten, that it's too hard to answer. So, I nod. That's the best I can do. And we are gone.

CHAPTER 19

We're not in the RACE building anymore. At least, I don't think we are. This place is made from grey bricks, no semblance of any decoration or prettiness. Cement floors, plain bricks, only a few windows high up in the wall to let in the moonlight.

'Where are we?'

'Under Charles's house.'

I step back, heart thumping. This is it. He's going to hand me over to Charles – this is what the agreement thing meant. Suck me in and then betray me!

'Jesus, Rhi. Will you stop it? I'm not turning you over to Charles. This is where Adam is.'

'I thought he was still at RACE.'

'Yeah, most of us did. Like I said, that was the rumour. But Charles brought me here. Only for a few minutes. That's why I couldn't come and get you. He wouldn't let me actually talk to Adam though. That's one of the reasons I wouldn't do what he asked.'

'Kill him?'

'Yeah.'

He walks forward to a plain, wooden door and looks at me for a second, like he's checking I'm okay – I'm so not, but that's beside the point. I need to do this. My hands are shaking and I stuff them in my pockets as he opens the door.

Adam is in a room within a room. I can't believe that Charles has him down here, like a caged animal. Bricked in, with only one window to see out...or in. He is pacing beside a bed. Back and forth, turning swiftly, like he has too much energy. His hair is slightly longer than from the few memories I have but it is the same shade as mine. Tall – obviously we don't share that gene. And still not smiling. My brother. It's hard to watch. I move from the window and try the door to his cell, but it's locked. Of course.

I go back to the glass. Josh is behind me and, selfishly, I'm glad he's here and I don't have to do this by myself.

'Why doesn't he just stream out of there?'

'Charles has rigged it so he can't. Electrical fields or something. Something that messes with his ability to stream.'

I want Adam to see me and I want to run away, all at the same time. It's too much – too hard – too real… I take a deep breath. Cowards suck. I knock on the window.

He turns so quickly, his face almost manic, that I actually take a step back before I can stop myself. But when I see his face, even with that crazed look, more memories rush back in to fill the spaces. Memories of Adam teaching me to ride a bike, being there when I cooked my first dinner, helping me to get control of my ability to stream…always being there for me…someone I could trust when everyone else had let me down.

He jabs his finger into a button at the side of the window and his voice comes out of a speaker under the glass.

'Rhi! What are you doing? You shouldn't be here.'

There's a button on my side too and I move forward to push it.

'I had to come and see you. We need to get you out of here.'

'No!' The word shoots out like a bullet. I shut my eyes for a moment, feeling the force of it in my body like it's a real thing, creating damage to my heart. When I open them again, he's still watching me.

'You have to leave. Now. Get away. If Dad finds you down here…' He shakes his head, and then shakes it again, like he's got someone else talking to him.

'Our father…!' I stop for a moment and take

another deep breath. 'Our father wants you dead! I can't leave you here.'

'Good. I should be.'

'Don't say that!' I put my hand against the glass. It leaves a print, like a ghost image. This is so not going how I thought it would. 'You're being stupid!'

He comes closer, right up to the glass, like he's trying to scare me. But my heart thumping in my chest is the only indication that it's working and he can't see that.

'You can't do anything here, Rhi. Now fuck off!'

I narrow my eyes at him and lean forward as well.

'Listen, I don't know what your problem is, but I'm not going anywhere. You're my brother. If you think I'm just going to walk away like a scared little girl and let you be killed by…well, by whoever Charles can convince to do it…then you don't know me very well.'

'Go away!'

'No!'

He just looks at me for a moment and then I watch the fight leaves his eyes. I don't like what's left. He lays his head against the window, his eyes closed. I want to rush in there and wrap him in my arms like he used to do to me. I can't stand that he's so sad – so lost – and my heart squeezes in on itself, trying to suffocate me.

'Please Rhi, just go. Josh, take her away.' He

sounds tired…worn out, like he's lost the will to fight.

I glance back at Josh but he's smart enough not to have moved. He nods and I turn back.

'I'm not going, Adam, so you can stop asking me to. Do you know where the key for the door is? We can take you away…somewhere Charles can't find you.'

He looks up at me and shakes his head.

'You can't. If you let me out, I'll kill you. You or someone else. It's happened before. I deserve to be dead.'

I think about the man at the lookout that's dead because of me, and the energy I've been taking from Josh without even trying to.

'You *can* control it. I know, because I've done it too. I killed someone.'

He steps back, away from the speaker, away from me. His eyes are wide. Scared? Of me? He sits on the bed, arms beside him, staring into space. He isn't looking at me anymore. It's as if I've disappeared and it's a punch to the stomach – a rejection of me; a judgment of what I've done from someone whose love I've never had to question. I blink away tears. Because this is not about me. This is about Adam and getting him out of here. Making him safe. I knock on the glass, wanting him to come back, but he ignores me. I turn to Josh.

'We need to find the key.'

Josh's eyes are sad. I want to slap him.

'It's no good. I know you think he's like you but he's not. He can't control it like you can.'

My hands are on my hips. 'Right. And you know this how?'

'Charles told me – '

'Oh yes, and Charles is so trustworthy.'

'Stop it. Listen to me. Adam's killed. Three times.'

'So have I or have you forgotten that.'

I'm staring at him, daring him to contradict me. He just shakes his head.

'It's not the same. You can control it. Adam can't. He can't stop once he's started. He doesn't stop draining energy until they're dead.'

'Bullshit! Charles just wants you to believe that.'

'It's not bullshit, Rhi.' He grabs my arms and swings me around so that I'm looking at my brother's cell again. 'Adam went in there by himself. He chose to do this! So he didn't hurt anyone else!'

My lips are thin lines – so thin they're starting to hurt. It can't be true. Josh just doesn't know how it feels, this draining energy thing. He doesn't understand. And he's so willing to believe Charles. But I know – I *know* my father can't be trusted, even if I don't know how I know that.

I don't answer him and I feel his arms drop away. He sighs like I'm the most immature, stubborn person in the world. So what? I don't care. Even if there's a part of me that wants his hands back. Even if the thought of him not being here with me is enough to make my stomach clench like I'm going to be sick. I need to do this for Adam. I need to show him I won't give up.

Adam is back at the glass, his eyes wild again. He presses the button for the speaker.

'What did he do to you?'

'Who?'

'Dad. Charles.'

'I don't…he didn't do anything.'

He stares at me.

'What. Did. He. Do.'

Josh leans past me and presses the button.

'She can't remember anything more than four days ago. Why?'

Adam looks from me to Josh and then back to me.

'I think he must have experimented on you too.'

For a moment, it feels like I can't breathe. My body is responding to what Adam's said even if my brain doesn't understand it. I grip the wood around the window, so tightly that it feels like I'm trying to sink my fingers into it.

'What does that mean – experimented?'

Adam drags his fingers down his cheeks, drawing his skin down like he's trying to scrape it off his skull. He talks as if he hasn't heard me. Like he's lost in his own world.

'I didn't mean for him to ever touch you. That's

not what was supposed to happen. You know that, right?'

I swallow. It's difficult. There's a lump in my throat the size of a tennis ball. I ask the question against my better judgment.

'What did he do, Adam?'

He shakes his head, like he's trying to find the words. I wait for him.

'After I became…like this, that was supposed to be the end. No more. It was too risky, even if it meant giving up the possibility of doing more than we ever could before. I'll kill him if he did this to you. I will. You know I'd never hurt you.'

The rhetoric is all well and good but it doesn't tell me what's happened – what my father did to me.

'What did he do?' The words come out harsher than I expected and he shuts his eyes. 'Tell me.'

'We'd got to thinking – Dad and I – about what more we could do with our abilities. How we could use them to make the world a better place.'

My snort interrupts him and he frowns at me. In that moment, he looks like the Adam I know and love.

'I can believe that of you maybe, but definitely not Dad.'

He nods, a slow one, like he's only just waking up to the facts. 'You could be right. If he's done this to you…'

'Just tell us Adam.' I can hear Josh's impatience.

'We've been using different things – medication, shock treatments, energy pulsing – to try to extend our abilities. Make us more effective. Be able to use our streaming in different ways.'

'Shock treatment. Jesus!' Josh's frown is back and he puts his hand on my shoulder like he's protecting me.

'When you say you want to use streaming in different ways, you mean being able to drain people's energy.'

'Yes.' He sighs. 'That's one of the possibilities. And to use this energy so that we don't have to sleep or eat. We can always be available. Helping the world.'

'Why? Why would you want to do that?'

'Think about it. The possibilities – terrible people in our world – we'd be able to go in and take them out without hurting anyone else. We'd be able to save people – hostages, innocent people being hurt by someone doing horrible things. Evil things.'

'We aren't Gods! How do you get to decide who lives and dies?'

'How do *they* get to decide that?' He looks manic again – his eyes shining, his face red. 'Imagine what good we could do in the world, Rhi. And how much people would pay us for things that they can't do themselves.'

'Jesus, you sound like Charles.'

He waves his hand. 'The money would be a side

benefit. The effect we could have on the world – that would be the pinnacle. That would be how we'd gauge our success.'

I shake my head. It's unbelievable. This is Adam. Adam! My caring, supportive, wonderful, older brother. The one I could always rely on. But maybe that's the reason he's done this – instead of just caring about me, he wants to care for the whole frigging world.

'Do you think Charles did this to me?'

Adam takes a minute before he nods his head. 'He must have. That's the only way this can be happening. He must've tried it with you because it didn't work the way we expected with me.'

'Jesus! He's experimenting on his own children. Fucking father of the year!' It's like an all-time low, even for the shitty father that he's been.

'I wanted him to do it to me though. I asked for it.'

'But I didn't!' At least, I don't think I did. No. It's not something I would have agreed to. Even if Adam thought it was a good plan, he wouldn't have convinced me. I'm sure of it.

'I don't know, Rhi. I don't want to imagine that he'd do that – not against your will.'

'Yeah, well, you've always seen Charles differently to me.' I don't tell him that he's wrong and I'm right. There doesn't seem any point. I knock on the wood. 'We need to get you out of here.'

'No!' He slams his hand on the window and I flinch. 'You can't do that. You don't understand. I can't control the energy flow. I can't stop it once it starts.'

I step forward – right up to the window – so that I can look into his eyes. So that he understands I mean business. 'I know you can do it. You taught me. Right back when my streamer abilities came along, you've been the one to teach me. If I've been able to control this new shit, you will be too. I believe in you.'

'No, I can't. I can't!'

But I'm not listening anymore. I move away from the window, searching for something I can use on the door handle. The fire extinguisher on the wall will have to do and I reef it out of its metal ring.

Josh grabs hold of it, stopping my swing as I go to bring it down on the metal.

'I don't think this is a good idea.'

I raise my eyebrows.

'I don't care what you think. This is my brother. I'm not leaving him in there.'

'Rhi…'

'Get out of my way Josh.'

He holds onto it for a moment longer and I wonder whether I'm going to actually have to knee him before he lets his hands drop.

'Be careful.'

I don't even bother to respond. The sound of

metal on metal echoes around the bare room and I cringe at the loudness of it. It takes three hits for the handle to break away and, by that time, I'm expecting someone to rush in. Charles, probably. That'd be my luck.

I push against the door and it gives way under my weight. Adam is sitting on the bed, curled up in the corner like he's trying to get as far away from me as possible. It makes my heart ache, like it's been squeezed through the hole of a needle. I walk towards the bed – slowly, trying not to make it worse for him.

'Adam, it's okay.'

But he's shaking his head – faster the closer I get until I'm afraid that he's going to do himself an injury.

'Adam.' I stretch out my hand, wanting the contact. Sure that he won't be able to hurt me – not when Charles has set up the room to stop him streaming out. Surely that will protect us.

And then it hits me. And I know I'm wrong. I go to my knees. I can't help it. He's taking my energy. All of it. Sucking me dry at an astonishing speed. I am flat on the floor before I know it. I can't get back up. I can't do anything. It's an onslaught – one that I have no answer to.

'No. No, no, no.' I can hear Adam, even if there's nothing I can do.

It's going dark. Although I don't think it really is. It's me going dark. Fading.

I only just register the sound of footsteps beside me. Josh! I want to yell at him to get out but I can't. It's too hard. I can't even grunt. There's the sound of something being thrown and, for a second, the power lets off. For a second, I can breathe.

And then Josh is there, at my head, helping me to sit up. I grab his arm.

'Leave me. Get out.'

'I'm not leaving you,' he says and that's all he has the opportunity to say before he too is on his knees. He grunts as he lands on the floor. I can feel the power, grabbing at me, trying to drain me again, but it's different this time. As if having two targets weakens it somehow. Only a little but enough that I can think. Enough that I can do something.

I push against the energy, trying to move it away from Josh but it doesn't work. It's too strong. I do the only other thing I can do. I reach out to Adam's energy which is blazing like a red fire, a mix of his energy and ours. And I pull it to me.

He gasps and looks at me.

'Yes. Take it. End it. Please, Rhi.'

I shake my head. I am not going to kill him. I am not going to have that hanging over me for the rest of my life. I look at Josh. He's pale. Going grey like the man on the lookout, barely breathing. Shit! I grab his hand, knowing that it isn't going to change anything but needing to have that physical contact. Josh, who tried to save me. Josh, who's been there for me, despite the poison Charles has spewed that's made me think otherwise. I concentrate, pulling just enough from Adam for him to start to sag…enough that his eyes roll back into his head. And then I let go.

I'm buzzing. Hyped up on energy. I could run a marathon and still be good for another one. I pull at Josh and he comes up to me like our sizes have reversed. He gasps for air and I take that as a good sign. I don't want to feel for his energy, just in case… well, just in case I can't control it.

The slow clapping from behind us has me turning so sharply I almost fall over.

It's Charles, standing there with a satisfied smirk on his face. I move forward to slap him before the gun in his hand stops me.

'What? Are you going to kill me now?'

He laughs and it makes me want to run. Run far from here and never come back. But Josh can't do that and I won't leave him. I can hear my heartbeat pounding in my ears.

'No, Rhiannon, I'm not going to kill you. What would be the point in that? You're everything we've worked for.'

I stand up as straight as I can and draw my shoulders back.

'Well then, you've done all of this for nothing.

Because I don't owe you anything. I don't want you anywhere near me. I don't want you to try and contact me. I don't care what sort of fucking scheme you had going with Adam, I'm not going to be a part of it.'

'Such language. I'm sure you got that from your mother.'

I ignore that, even though it's hard. Because I want to scream at him, ask where the hell he was for my whole childhood to be worried about my language now. But I need to pick my battles and, right at this moment, I'm glad he wasn't there when I was a kid, otherwise there's a good chance I'd be more screwed up than I am now.

'Did you force this on me? Did you do your stupid experiments, like Adam said?'

'So you did lose your memory!' He chuckles to himself. Chuckles! Who does that? I can't believe I'm related to him. 'Force is such an ugly word. Let's just say I persuaded you.'

'Persuaded me how?'

He glances at Josh.

'It's amazing what you'll do when someone threatens a person you care for.'

And then, like a row – no, a frigging field of dominoes – falling into place, it comes back to me. My memories slot together like they're a reward for getting to this place. I remember loving Josh, even though my head was telling me I should protect myself. I remember the threat from Charles, forcing me to take the medications and be strapped down to a bed to have electricity pumped into my body, for God's sake! The effects of it all – the shakes and the sickness and forgetting things. How hard it was to keep it from Josh; scared of what he'd do if he knew. And then breaking it off from him, even though it broke me with it, trying to protect him and stop Charles at the same time. Stop what he was doing to me, to us, to Adam. And yet, it didn't stop.

I remember being strapped to the bed and realising that this would never end, not until Charles killed me like he was killing Adam, all in the name of money. No, not money…power. And I remember streaming out, even though it shouldn't have been possible with the electrodes attached to my head. Streaming out and getting away. But obviously losing my memory in the process.

'You'll never get the chance to do that to me again.'

'We'll see. You're much stronger than I suspected, steaming out like that. Stronger than Adam maybe, given that you were able to withstand the draining despite the fact that you're related. We'll need to talk more about that. But there's something I have to do first.'

He walks over to the bed and stands there for a second, looking at Adam. And then he brings up the gun …and fires.

I react too late. By the time I go to move forward, there's already a red stain spreading over my brother's chest. I'm frozen. Paralysed. Except for my heart, which is pounding against my rib cage, wanting to move forward even though my body can't.

Not Adam. No. It can't be possible. No. No!

'Now that's done…'

I swing to Charles, face hot, muscles bunched together like steel cables.

'What the fuck have you done?' I scream the words at him but he just watches me like he thinks I'm being stupid. Like I'm overreacting. It's surreal. I don't know what to do, what to say. So I scream the obvious. 'He was your son!'

'Yes, and I *am* sad. Very sad. He was a great support to me. A good son. But it needed to be done. We needed to be practical about this. He wasn't stable and he wanted it to end. I was merely the tool that finished what you started – the perfect opportunity to finish it given that you'd rendered his ability useless. Thank you.'

My eyes are so wide in my head that they feel like they're going to pop out of their sockets. Me! He's putting it on me! Saying that I'm a part of Adam's death!

'You bastard!'

'Rhiannon, always so melodramatic. Did he not just try and kill you and the man you love?'

I shake my head, refusing to agree with him. I

will never do that. I can't. If I do, I'm lost. 'I could have helped him! And you did this to him in the first place. You made him like this!'

'Yes, and I wish it could have been avoided. But you couldn't have helped him. Nothing we did was reversing the effects. It was only a matter of time before we needed to end it for him. He knew that. It was a mercy killing really.'

The rage pulses in me like a living being, wanting to hurt something.

Someone.

Him.

I pull at his energy, urging it to come to me like filings to a magnet, and it's his turn to look surprised. Maybe he didn't think his darling daughter had it in her. Well, he was wrong.

He turns the gun to me but his fingers are shaking and I know he probably can't control it enough to shoot me. Not that I care if he does. I'm past that. All I want is him gone. Gone, gone, gone!

He drops the gun and still I don't stop. Still I pull his energy to me, draining him, leaving him with nothing. Even when he falls to the floor, I don't flinch. I have a purpose and it's to see this man dead. He has taken too much from me already – a normal childhood, a father to love me, my memory, the brother who was my only real family. He's not taking anymore.

Josh's touch is the only thing that intrudes on my

mission. He's recovered, enough to be able to stand and wrap his arm around my waist.

'Rhiannon, stop it.'

'No.'

'Rhi, please, you don't want to do this. Don't let him make you like him.'

I waver, not pulling back but slowing the drain.

'I don't think I can. I want him dead.'

He puts his fingers around my chin and turns my face so that I'm looking at him.

'Please. Stop it. Don't be the person he's forcing you to be. For me. I love you.'

'Even now? Even when I'm capable of this.'

'Always.'

I let the energy go. Charles isn't dead. He's gasping for air, face grey, but he's alive. I move out of Josh's embrace and go over to my father.

'Don't try to find me. Don't try to contact me. I want nothing to do with you. Ever.'

'You'll come back.' His voice is soft and hoarse, like it's an effort to talk. 'This isn't the end. You'll need me.'

'In your dreams.'

He shakes his head. 'You don't know yet. You'll be back.'

But I'm sick of his mind games. I'm not doing this anymore. I'm tired of this stupid dance. I turn away. Turn away and see Josh. Waiting for me. The man I trust. The man I know I love. I take his hand and he smiles. A gentle one. One just for me.

'Come on.'

I look back again. I want to take Adam's body – want to make sure that Charles doesn't touch him ever again but my father is standing between us, and I'm not taking the chance of getting closer to him, despite what I know I can do. Or maybe because of it. Josh is right – I don't want to sink to his level. Adam would understand, I know he would. I tell myself that he'd even be proud that I'm making this decision and not angry that I'm leaving him here. I hope I'm right. But it doesn't stop my heart crumbling to bits as I walk away.

It's only when we're out of the cell that I hear movement. It startles me and I spin, expecting to see Charles there again, gun pointed at us, ready to end us both. But he's still in the cell. I can see through the window. He's standing up, watching us go. The scowl on his face makes him look like he hates me. Maybe he does. I don't care. I'm not wasting any more emotion on him.

But because he's looking at me, he doesn't see Adam on the bed behind him. He doesn't see him raise his head. It takes a second for that to hit me. Adam! He's not dead! I turn, ready to go back in – I don't know what I think I'm going to do; all I know is that I have to go to him. Be there for him like he's been there for me so many times. But Josh grabs my hand, holding me. And I understand why. Because Charles is collapsing again, the colour leaching out of him, each spasm getting weaker, until his eyes are wide open, staring at me but not seeing me.

Adam nods. Just once. A confirmation of his love before his head falls back on the bed. And then he too is staring, unseeing. Gone from me. The sob escapes me before I even realize I'm crying. And then Josh is wrapping me in his arms again. Holding me. And we are gone.

EPILOGUE

The house overlooks the lake. It's quiet and peaceful and beautiful. And when we need more action in our life, we stream out, going wherever we want in the world. Josh and I. My husband. I have committed. I trust him. With everything.

With both Charles and Adam dead, I am the sole recipient of their wealth. And although initially, I didn't want any of it, I've decided I deserve it. I deserve to rebuild the life that Charles tried to ruin in order to get what he wanted. I deserve to try to be normal. As normal as streamers can be anyway. So we've kept enough to buy the house and continue to live on and I've used the rest to set up a charity for children who have suffered abuse. Giving something back.

I stretch in the chair and rub my belly.

'How's she going?'

I smile at Josh.

'*He's* going fine.'

He laughs and bends down to kiss me and then kiss my growing stomach.

I look out over the water, refusing to worry. It's an effort but I'm getting better. It was a shock to find out I was pregnant a month after breaking free from Charles. Two months pregnant almost. I'm sure this is what he meant when he told me there was something I didn't know yet. Why he was sure I'd be back. Shows you how much he knew me. Even with this, there's no way I'd go back, even if I could.

We managed to persuade the doctor who worked for Charles in his 'experimental' work to give us information. It wasn't too hard. Threatening him with disbarment worked a charm, thank God. I didn't want to have to take his energy in order to force him. I don't want to ever have to do that again.

He told us that it's Josh's baby. Our baby. That Josh was drugged and the sperm unknowingly taken from him and used to impregnate me during one of the experiments. Because, apparently, Charles was sure that with the changes in my abilities and with Josh's normal streaming abilities, the baby would be everything he'd hoped. The next generation to carry out the work he yearned to do. To give him the power he wanted.

As if I'd ever give him my baby, regardless of how the pregnancy came about.

I don't care. It is our baby. And we will raise him or her with every ounce of love that we have to give. We will fill our lives with love and trust and family. And we will be happy.

THE END

AFTERWORD

I hope you enjoyed *Streamer*. A million thanks to you, the reader, for taking the plunge with Rhiannon and Josh.

Author's souls are nourished by reviews so if you feel so inclined, I'd love to hear what you think.

Want to read more? Read on for the first chapter of *Blue* by Sue-Ellen Pashley.

BLUE BY SUE-ELLEN PASHLEY

This is what I know about me for sure.

I am seventeen.

I am a twin.

And I am an invader of homes. A thief who takes people's things, including their peace of mind. It's not what I want to do. It's not who I want to be. But I don't have a choice.

I stare out the window of the car, head on my palm. I can feel the vibrations of the road through my elbow, resting on the door sill. Every bump nearly slams my head into the window, but I don't move. Maybe I can knock myself out. Then I won't have to think.

This town looks like every other one we've been to. House after house, all of them basically the same, everyone living their normal, ordinary lives. We've been to so many of these little nothing towns now, I'm starting to lose track. Just once, I'd like to go somewhere where things are different. Not just the town, but our lives too. A normal, ordinary life – that's what I want.

Not that there's any chance of that.

I glance over at Gep. He's concentrating so hard on the road it looks like he's trying to make it bend to his will. His dark hair is grey at the edges and the lines on his face look like they've well and truly settled in. Weathered, I think they call it. He's looked like this for as long as I can remember. I think it's because we've moved around so much that we're the only ones who realise he never seems to age…

I watch him, making sure I keep my face void of emotion, and try to work out when I actually started to hate him. Not just be scared of him but actually hate him. A hate that's a churning anger, deep in my gut, gnawing at me. Probably when I was fourteen. When he really started to take it out on Jimmy. When he showed how much of a sadistic bastard he is. Three years of burning rage with no way to get rid of it. Can't be good for my health.

He looks over at me, the lines in his forehead furrowing deeper.

'What the fuck's wrong with you?'

I look away, not stupid enough to answer, and stick my earphones in, letting the music wash over me, fill up my brain. My eyes shut out the bright, noon-day light. For a moment, I can pretend I'm somewhere else; pretend I'm some*one* else. The beat pounds in my ears, taking me away, drowning out my life.

The tap on my shoulder brings me back to reality. I pretend to ignore it, even though now it's all I can think about. When I feel the second tap, I know there's no point in continuing the sham. I reef an earphone out and twist in my seat. Jimmy's grinning at me, his green eyes bright, his blond hair all messed and sticking up like a frigging halo around his head. I can't help but grin back. He's the only one who can do that to me.

'What?'

'Do you think there'll be cute girls?'

The words slur out of his mouth and I can see he's trying hard not to let his left arm fly into Fox, sitting next to him. Not that he can help any of it. Brain damage from the car accident that killed our mum left him like this. That's what Gep's told me anyway. God knows if it's true. Not that it matters. He's my brother. My twin. It's as simple as that.

'Yeah, and they'll all be flocking around, running their fingers through your hair, trying to do things for you, make things easier. Frigging underdog shit always works.'

He grins at me again and turns to Fox.

'Did you hear that?' he says. 'Penn reckons I'm going to outplay you again.'

Fox shakes his head, his red hair a fiery mess in the sun.

'You're a freak, man. God, makes me sick the way the girls want to talk to you all the time.'

'You're just jealous,' I say. 'He can't help it if he's got normal coloured hair and the girls can't work out if you're a guy or a monkey.'

'Fuck you,' he says, but there's no real feeling to it. He doesn't want to be here anymore than I do.

'It's a pointless conversation anyway.' Gep's voice is loud in the car, dominating the space around us. 'Jimmy's not going to school this time.'

My heart sinks, spiralling down like it's not controlled by my body anymore, making me nauseous. Not again. Not after last time.

'That's shit,' I say.

I know I should keep my mouth shut – in fact, every cell in my body is begging me to do just that – but my anger makes me stupid.

He looks over at me, eyes narrowed.

'What did you say?'

I take a deep breath. The other boys in the car – Jimmy, Fox and Kat – are silent. I can feel them watching me; feel their tension. And I know if I turned around to look at Jimmy, his eyes would be telling me to shut up. But I can't. The words spew out of my mouth like I'm a suicidal moron.

'I said that's shit. He should be able to go to school. I'll do what you want me to do. You don't have to worry about it, alright? I'll do it.'

'Damn right you'll do it. But after the little… rebellion you had last time, Jimmy's my insurance. So, you'd better be a good boy.'

He leans over to pat my cheek like I'm five years old. I try not to jerk away at his touch but it's hard. He smirks, like he knows. It's that smirk that does my head in. I whack his hand away with my forearm.

'Fucking psycho.'

It's muttered under my breath but I know he'll hear it. Even then, I'm not ready for what he does next. You'd think I would be. After living with him, day in and day out, for the last sixteen years, you'd think I'd be able to predict his actions.

But he moves so quickly, I don't react until his hand is on the bare skin of my arm. And I know what's going to happen, even if I don't know how he does it. I feel his energy burning into me, coursing through my body, like it's charring my veins, leaving only ash in its wake. It takes all of my strength to not scream out, even though it feels like my whole body is on fire, the heat engulfing me, burning every organ to a crisp, until I'm just a shell. But I keep it in, not giving him the satisfaction, like I've done so many times before. And, even more important than that, not letting Jimmy hear it – not putting him through that.

It seems to go on and on, until there's only the heat, the burn.

I hear Jimmy yell out and it's the last thing I hear before the blackness takes me.

ABOUT THE AUTHOR

A writer of copious amounts of words – just because if they didn't come out, she's sure they'd make her head explode – Sue-Ellen is an international author with seven published YA and adult stories: *Aquila, When Henry Met Gina, The Jade Goddess, Streamer, The Flight, Talon Marked* and *The Rise*, with her children's picture book, *The Jacket*, released in Australia, UK and the US.

In her 'other' life, Sue-Ellen is a social worker living in Central Queensland with her family, two dogs, a bird and a snake. A lover of tea, wine, chocolate and slightly weird shoes, she's an eternal optimist who enjoys making things difficult for her protagonists but loves a satisfying ending.

She loves to connect with readers and you can find her on facebook, goodreads or at www.sueellenpashley.com.

ALSO BY SUE-ELLEN PASHLEY

Aquila

Streamer

The Rise

Blue

Short Stories

When Harry Met Gina

Bad Guy

Talon Marked

Children's Books

The Jacket

Ingram Content Group UK Ltd.
Milton Keynes UK
UKHW020703130723
425065UK00016B/375